I0664636

MURDER AT THE MARS CLUB

FROM THE MURDER ON MARS SERIES

By Greg Fowlkes

Includes a special preview of

THE BLOOD RED SANDS OF MARS PART ONE FROM THE MURDER ON MARS SERIES

MURDER AT THE MARS CLUB

© 2016 The Fictional Press
www.TheFictionalPress.com

All rights reserved. No part of this book may be used or reproduced in any manner without written permission except for brief quotations for review purposes.

Published by The Fictional Press

The Fictional Press, an imprint of Intrepid Ink, LLC, provides full publishing services to authors of fiction and non-fiction books, eBooks and websites. From editing to formatting, to publishing, to marketing, Intrepid Ink gets your creative works into the hands of the people who want to read them.

Find out more at www.thefictionalpress.com.

ISBN 13: 978-1-943403-27-1

Printed in the United States of America

BOOKS BY GREG FOWLKES

From the Wizard at Law Series:
The Laws of Magic
Trial by Magic

From the Murder on Mars Series:
Blood Red Sands of Mars
A Death at Station Alpha
A Corpse in Hut Town
Murder at the Mars Club

From the Fictional Detective Series:
The Fictional Detective
A Fictional Detective Trifecta

Star City Stories: Space Opera Noir Featuring Frank Sladek

The Uncorrupted Corpse

Tequila Visions

Cargo From Paradise

Ice Viking

TABLE OF CONTENTS

CHAPTER 1
"THE UNPLEASANTNESS AT THE MARS CLUB"

From appearances, one would not have guessed that the interior of the room had never come closer than fifty million kilometers to London, or for that matter, anywhere else on Earth, but then, the Mars Club had been modeled on the ideal of a London Gentlemen's Club of the first half of the twentieth century, and the Lounge Room was no exception to that model. From the oiled walnut paneling, so different than the fused silica blocks, aluminum struts and plastic sheeting typical of Martian construction, to the over-stuffed leather armchairs whose padding was so unnecessary in the planet's reduced gravity, no expense had been spared in creating an illusion for that small group of men who were actually responsible for running the planet.

The lounge, as with the rest of the club, had been decorated in the Art Deco style, a style that had been the height of modernity in, oh say the 1930's. The lighting was muted and provided by lamps and wall sconces of brushed aluminum with the sleek curves of that era. In addition to the armchairs, the room had been furnished with side tables and other fixtures appropriate to the purpose of the room, which was to provide a retreat for the club's select membership. A built in bookcase along one wall contained a tasteful selection of bound volumes. As a concession to the late twenty first century a large video display was set into another wall and was tuned to the WorldNet news feed, though, by club policy, the sound was always turned off except during times of political or financial crisis. The one curious aspect of the room was that it had no windows, for the Mars Club, as with all permanent construction on the planet, was buried underground in order to provide the protection from radiation that the thin atmosphere did not.

The Mars Club was the sanctuary for the resident heads of the great mining operations that formed the basis of the Martian economy, men like Stanley Olberman, the manager of operations for Transamerican Minerals, Leo Kichler, local director of Rio Plata Mining, Wu Lin, the local factor for The Peoples Celestial Mineral Corporation, or Helmut Nordlund of Interplanetary Transport who managed the fleet of spaceships that formed the vital connecting link with the mother planet. It was a place where, for at least a short time, these men could enjoy all the comforts of home. For Mars at the tail end of the twenty-first century was still considered a hardship posting, a Spartan outpost to be endured, a planet still dominated by fragile pneumatic architecture, where a surface suit and life support pack were required before one could step outside, and most of life's luxuries and many of the necessities had to be imported at great expense from Earth.

With a few exceptions, the men in the lounge that night were short timers on Mars. They were men on the way up in their respective corporations, posted to Mars for a tenure of one or two years as a way to broaden their resumes and prove their competency before making the final step to top management. They were intelligent, educated, cosmopolitan men. In addition to training in finance, most held degrees in engineering or geology. They had come up through the ranks of their respective companies, often serving their apprenticeships in some of the harshest environments that Earth offered, for by the end of the twenty-first century mineral wealth was rarely to be found in comfortable locations.

As was common, the members of the Mars Club had retired to the lounge after dinner. Unlike the typical utilitarian Martian attire, they were dressed in suits and ties, perhaps the only persons on Mars to wear the latter, though the customs and rules of the Mars Club did not extend to requiring dinner jackets except on the most formal of occasions. A party of four were playing bridge at a table off to one side of the room and indulging in snifters of fine California brandy or single malt Scotch that had actually been distilled over a peat fire and aged in wood casks in a warehouse Speyside. The click of balls could be heard coming from the billiard's room, but it didn't seem to be disturbing the two members who had positioned themselves in a pair of armchairs to read.

Into this scene a man entered, to take up a position in front of and just to one side of one of the readers. He was impeccably groomed, his trousers creased to crisp perfection, his shoes polished till they shined. He waited silently until he was noticed.

Amongst the members of the Mars club, Otis McAndrews was an anomaly. He was a long time resident of the planet, having served as the local head of Anglo-Martian Mining for nearly twenty years. One of the pioneers of the rare-earth mining boom, he had spent so much time on the planet that the doctors had told him that a return to the higher gravity of Earth might well prove fatal. While other men might have lamented this sentence, McAndrews had accepted it with stoicism and thrown himself into both his work and efforts to make Mars a better place for all that lived there. By virtue of his seniority he had been chosen Secretary of the Club, a post that he had held since the inception of that institution.

Looking up at the newcomer he asked, "Yes, Fenton, what is it?" his tone in no way betraying irritation at being interrupted.

Howard Fenton, the club steward and manager replied with all the deference he was capable of, "I'm sorry to bother you, sir, but I'm afraid there is a matter requiring your attention."

McAndrews was more intrigued than annoyed. Fenton was far too competent a manager to bother him with trivialities. "Well, what is it?"

"I'd rather not go into it here, sir. If you could come with me?"

McAndrews set down his book and stood up, following the steward into the hallway. He found himself being led up the staircase to the second floor of the club which was occupied by suites of rooms for those members who chose to reside in the club. They did not stop at any of these chambers however, but instead they took yet another flight of stairs upward.

"It's Mr. Krieger, sir. I'm afraid something has happened to him," Fenton said as he paused at the top of the stairs to operate the controls of an airlock.

"What do you mean, Fenton? Why are you being so mysterious?"

"I'm not exactly sure, Mr. McAndrews. That's why I thought I should fetch you." His tone indicated that he was only too willing to allow someone else to take responsibility for the matter.

The airlock door swung open to reveal what was probably the most remarkable room on the planet. Above them the heavens seemed to open out. The Cupola, as it was known, consisted of a circular chamber some ten meters in diameter covered by a glass dome looking out into a Martian sky which was just descending into twilight.

The dome was supported by a low wall, thus allowing a 360 degree view of the surrounding Martian landscape. Off in the distance to the west McAndrews could see the lights of the spaceport, while the heavy industrial district was visible over to the east. Of Mars City proper, of which they were almost in the center, there was very little to be seen, buried as it was under a half meter of radiation shielding soil. Not for the first time, McAndrews noted that a carefully placed berm of sand concealed most of what was known as Hut Town, the original settlement of inflatable buildings now occupied by those catering to the low tastes of miners in town for a spree or those looking for cheaper rents. What McAndrews knew, but which few others realized, was that the berm served no other purpose.

The Cupola was used on rare occasions for parties and receptions, though most of the members found it a bit chilly, and preferred the comforts of the lounge below, the dome serving as a reminder of how fragile was man's presence on Mars. With one exception, that was. That exception was Peter Krieger. McAndrews did not find it at all unusual to discover Krieger in the Cupola after dinner. Krieger was that oddity, a smoker, rare enough these days on Earth, but almost unheard of on Mars. He seemed to require a cigar after dinner, and by tacit agreement he would retire to the Cupola for a cigar and a glass of port when the others adjourned to the lounge or billiard room. The air filters in the Cupola were quite capable of eliminating the smoke and the smell never penetrated to the rooms below.

True to form, it would seem that Krieger had come up to the Cupola to sit and enjoy his cigar while he watched the Martian sunset. The stub of the cigar was resting, still smoldering, in the ashtray on the table next to him. A half consumed glass of port sat next to the ashtray.

Krieger himself was in the chair. It was also quite evident that he was dead. There was a horrible expression on his face and his eyes were wide open, staring blankly at nothing.

To make sure, McAndrews felt for a pulse, though he knew it was in vain.

"He is dead, sir, isn't he?" Fenton asked.

"Yes. Quite dead."

"What should we do, sir?"

McAndrews picked up the port glass by the stem and sniffed at the contents.

"We must contact McKernan," McAndrews stated grimly.

"The Chief Inspector?" Fenton asked.

"Yes, the Chief Inspector. I'm afraid, Fenton, that Mr. Krieger has been murdered."

"Do you mean—?"

"Yes. The port has been poisoned." Seeing the look of horror on the steward's face McAndrews reassured him, "Don't worry, Fenton. I'll contact the inspector myself. In the mean time, don't disturb anything, and don't let anyone up into the Cupola until the inspector gets here. Do you understand?"

"Yes, sir."

CHAPTER 2
A QUIET DINNER INTERRUPTED

Though separated by less than a kilometer from the confines of the Mars Club, the space where Chief Inspector McKernan dined with Dr. Elisabeth Hastert couldn't have been more different. There was no pretense that it being anything other than what it was, a residence repurposed out of the old pneumatic structures that were the remnants of the first days of the original settlement on the planet. Designed for easy erection, the buildings of Hut Town consisted of little more than a thin skin of aluminized film which had been inflated, then stiffened with a layer of sprayed on insulation. When more permanent and substantial buildings had been constructed to house the corporations and the operations of the Trust Authority, the huts had been abandoned only to be re-occupied by those looking for cheap space in which to live and work.

McKernan's hut was more luxurious than most. He had first moved to Hut Town early during his first three year contract as head of security on Mars, in search of more space and privacy than was afforded by the bachelor quarters of the Trust Authority housing. Amenities had been spartan at first, but over the years he had improved and remodeled the hut to make it more comfortable. His biggest coup had been the acquisition of the adjoining hut which he had joined to the first with a recycled airlock. Not only had this allowed for a separate sleeping area, but it also provided redundancy to his life support system, something that was always appreciated by long term Martians.

Over the years he had furnished his hut with a variety of salvaged, recycled, and repurposed parts and fittings. What it lacked in aesthetics it made up for in comfort, a rare commodity on mankind's latest frontier. Despite the hut's origins, there were a few non-utilitarian items decorating the interior, a water-color marsscape that hung above the sofa and an odd amorphous sculpture that had been carved from a piece of metal exposed to the windblown dust of the Martian surface. Over the last year a few feminine touches had appeared since the doctor had taken to sharing the space.

The meal, as all too many had lately, proceeded in silence. An unspoken subject hung over the table, discouraging conversation on any other topic lest it turn to that discussion of which too much had been said already. The doctor was nearing the end of her three year contract, and as of yet had not made the decision to renew for another three years and remain on Mars or to return to Earth. For McKernan, there was no such choice to be made. After seven years on Mars he was committed to staying. He knew there was no place for him on the mother planet.

It wasn't that the doctor wasn't attracted to the ruggedly handsome man sitting across the table from her. He was brave, intelligent and had even proved to be amusing in those moments when he was relaxing away from his job as the head of the small police force the U.N. Trust Authority maintained to provide a semblance of law and order on Mars. But she knew from the experiences of others that those who signed up for a second three year contract on Mars rarely returned to Earth. She wasn't sure that she was willing to give up forever the greens and blues of the home planet and the free flowing air, however polluted, of Earth for life in a 'tin-can' where one could never step outside on the surface without wearing a surface suit. More importantly, she wasn't sure she was ready to raise a family under those circumstances. She knew that Erik wanted her to stay, but the decision was hers, and hers alone. Furthermore it was one that she would have to make in the next few months, and as that deadline approached the tensions in their relationship had grown steadily.

The diners were saved from having to deal with this subject by the beeping of McKernan's communicator. The inspector took a quick look at the display to read the identity of the caller.

"It's Otis McAndrews," he explained.

The doctor was surprised. While she had met the head of Anglo-Martian on a number of occasions, they hardly moved in the same circles. She knew that Erik had had dealings with him in the course of several cases and looked to him for support against the bureaucracy of the Trust Authority, but she saw that he was as surprised as she at the call.

"McKernan here. What can I do for you, sir?"

After a pause while McAndrews spoke, McKernan replied, "I see. I don't suppose you'd could tell me the nature of the problem."

"I understand. I'm at home right now, but I should be there in ten minutes or so. Do you want me to send a constable?"

"No? I understand, sir. I'll be there as soon as possible," the inspector said before disconnecting. Despite the lack of explanation from McAndrews, the seriousness of the matter was written on his face.

"I'm afraid I have to leave. There's been an incident at the Mars Club," McKernan explained to the doctor.

"An incident? What kind? I didn't think that anything ever happened at the Mars Club beyond the occasional corked bottle of wine." After a moment she added, "Will I be needed at the hospital?"

"I don't know. Otis was being very secretive, which is unlike him. He didn't want to talk about it over an open channel. But I don't think it's life threatening. I offered to send a constable, but he said that wouldn't be necessary for the moment."

"That *is* strange," the doctor responded.

"Yeah. Otis isn't the kind of man to overreact. He wouldn't have called me personally unless it was important. Or sensitive."

"Well, you have to go. I'll clean up."

"Thanks. You probably shouldn't wait up. There's no telling how long this may take."

He stood up and went to the side table where he picked up a small 5 mm. automatic pistol and clipped it to his belt. That was another thing that the doctor wasn't sure she was ready for. Erik was a policeman and Mars held dangers beyond accident and the hostile environment. He reached down and kissed her gently on the forehead before heading towards the airlock that served as their front door.

CHAPTER 3
"A WHIFF OF DEATH"

By intention, the entrance to the Mars Club was unremarkable. A standard air lock hatch was set into the fused silicon block wall of the "Grande Concourse", the rather pretentiously named main corridor of Mars City, which looked like nothing so much as the interior of a second rate shopping mall on Earth. The Mars Club was flanked on either side by the Mars Hotel and the Mars Sheriton, both of which presented a much flashier façade to those few travelers to Mars in search of temporary accommodations. These travelers were often puzzled at the blank space of wall between the two hotels broken only by the single hatch. To one side of this hatch there was a small plaque of polished brass which had been engraved with the two words "Mars Club." Just below the plaque was a small button.

It was this button which Chief Inspector Erik McKernan pressed as he faced the airlock hatch. He knew that there was a small camera hidden in the mechanism of the hatch which was used to screen those seeking entry to the sanctum of the Mars Club. He also knew that club members were given wireless devices that allowed them to bypass the screening, but he was not privileged enough to possess such a device.

He was not surprised when the hatch swung open a few seconds later. The hatch of the Mars Club, unlike most airlock hatches on Mars which were manually operated, was automatic, requiring no human intervention except for the operation of the control at the reception desk in vestibule of the club. The inspector stepped into the lock, waited for the outer door to close behind him and the inner hatch to open. As both the corridor outside and the interior of the Mars Club were at the same pressure, this protocol wasn't strictly necessary, but Mars being Mars, those residents who survived any period of time tended to be cautious with such matters.

Waiting for the inspector in the vestibule was Fenton, the club steward. McKernan had met this individual before on his rare visits to the Mars Club (he was not a member), but knew relatively little about him. Noting the impeccable dress of the latter, McKernan, who was dressed casually in jeans and a light sweater, felt out of place, but then, he always felt that way within the confines of the Mars Club.

"The Secretary would like to speak to you in the Cupola. If you will please follow me, Chief Inspector?" Fenton said in that voice reserved to butlers, maitre'd's and others holding similar positions.

"Just what is this about, Fenton?" McKernan asked, unconsciously slipping into the appropriate form of address.

"I believe Mr. McAndrews can explain better than I, sir. If you will follow me?"

There didn't seem to be any point in arguing the matter. McKernan followed the steward out of the vestibule and into the corridor that ran to the left towards the back of the club. To one side he could see the billiard room through a pair of doors. He noted in passing, that these doors, while faced in wood could be closed to form an air tight seal, a reminder that, all appearances to the contrary, he was still on Mars. Farther along the corridor another doorway opened to the lounge. He knew from past visits that to the right of the vestibule was another similar corridor off of which were the library and main dining room. The back of the club was occupied by a series of smaller rooms suitable for meetings, private dining, and other occasions as needed. In the space behind the vestibule between these two corridors was a small bar, a cozy, dimly lit space with a few small tables, several comfortable chairs and a settee. There were no stools in front of the bar. It was not that sort of establishment. Besides, this being Mars, standing in the lower gravity posed no great hardship.

Fenton led him past these areas to a staircase leading upwards. McKernan had never been to the second floor of the club, but he knew that it was taken up by suites and rooms for those members who chose to reside at the club or who stayed there while in transit. They did not pause on the second floor, though, but proceeded up a second flight of stairs.

McKernan had once been invited to a reception in the Cupola. He had found the space both exhilarating and a bit frightening. It was remarkable for the essentially unobstructed view that it provided of the Martian surface, a view that one normally could see only through the visor of the helmet of a surface suit or the viewing port of a Mars buggy. By its very nature, though, such a view produced a feeling of unease in anyone who, as had the inspector, spent years on Mars, and was all too aware of how things could go wrong in a hurry on a planet where the atmospheric pressure would be considered a fair vacuum on Earth.

McKernan did his best to ignore this feeling as they passed through the hatch into the Cupola, focusing instead on the tableau before him. What he saw was a man in his late fifties slumped down in a chair. Another man, somewhat older stood nearby, not quite at attention. The word 'distinguished' didn't adequately describe him. In another age one might easily have assumed he was a retired colonel in her majesty's service. He certainly looked the part with his iron gray hair, neatly trimmed moustache, and trim build. Though not above average height, he had the air of one used to issuing orders. He also looked as though, despite his years, he was quite capable of taking care of himself.

Otis McAndrews was, in some ways, the most powerful man on Mars. He had spent thirty-five years as a mining engineer working everywhere from Africa to the Arctic before being posted to Mars as head of operations for Anglo-Martian Mining. That had been nearly twenty years earlier. He had never left Mars, and now never would. As head of one of the most successful of the companies extracting rare-earths from Mars he was respected even by his competitors for both his intelligence and honesty. Over the years these traits had resulted in his coming to be viewed as the spokesman for all the commercial concerns on Mars in their dealings with the Trust Authority.

He was also a man that McKernan, despite the differences in their positions, considered his friend.

"You can leave us now, Fenton," McAndrews ordered. "I'll let you know if we need anything. And please see that no one comes up to the Cupola without the Inspector's permission."

"I take it he's dead?" McKernan asked.

"Yes, I'm afraid so, Erik." Noting the use of his first name, McKernan relaxed a bit.

"Fenton?"

"Yes, Inspector?"

"Have any of the members that were present tonight left?"

"Only the governor, sir. I'm not sure that the other members are quite aware of what has happened tonight, sir. Though if any of them noticed you—"

"Please gather them in the lounge and inform them that I will be down shortly to make an announcement."

"Very good, Inspector."

After the steward left McKernan asked "Who is he?" The face was unfamiliar to him. Mostly he dealt with the actual miners, not the executives.

"Peter Krieger. Head of Pretoria Mining. The whole thing, by the way, not just the operations here on Mars."

"A bit unusual that, isn't it?"

"Krieger wasn't the kind of man to delegate. He built Pretoria up from its very beginning. I gather that he saw Mars as being crucial to the future of the company. Therefore his presence. He was in the habit of splitting his time between here and Earth."

McKernan grunted in response. Given the amount of time travel between the two planets took, people who shuttled back and forth were rare. He filed the fact away and returned to the business at hand. "How was he discovered?"

"Jeeves, the butler, discovered him when he came up to check to see if he needed anything. He informed Fenton who then informed me. I called you."

"Jeeves?" McKernan questioned.

"I know it's silly. His real name is Watson. Somewhere along the line one of the members started calling him Jeeves and the nickname stuck. He doesn't appear to mind."

"Any idea of the cause of death?"

"I'd say he was poisoned," McAndrews stated. "My guess is cyanide. In the port."

"Just how would you know that, Otis?"

"I smelled the glass. It smelled of bitter almonds, the classic tell-tale of cyanide."

"Out of curiosity just how would you happen to know that?"

"Remember, I was a mining engineer for years, Erik. Cyanide is used extensively in mining and metallurgy."

"So it would be readily available on Mars?" With nearly everything having to be imported from Earth this was not an idle question.

"Oh, I suspect so. There's probably tons of the stuff laying around."

"Lovely," McKernan said in exasperation. "Is there anything you can tell me about the time of death."

"He ate dinner along with the rest of us. That was at eight. Sorry, 2000. We tend to be a bit old fashioned when in the Mars Club. Dinner ended around nine. People retired to the lounge or the billiard room. Krieger came up here to the Cupola as was his habit. He liked to smoke a cigar after dinner along with his port, and this is the only place he could do so without offending people. It was a long standing arrangement which he followed most nights."

"And he was discovered when?"

"Jeeves can tell you better than I can, but he told Fenton as soon as he discovered the body. Fenton immediately came to fetch me. I called you straight-away as soon as I saw the body, so it was probably no more than ten minutes or so before that."

"Did you touch anything?" McKernan asked.

"I'm afraid I did, Erik. I held his wrist to check for a pulse. I also picked up the glass by the stem, as well when I smelled it."

"Just why did you do that again?"

"I had my suspicions. It was the grimace on his face. I've seen it before, you see. Long ago. In Africa. I wasn't thinking. I just picked up the glass. Sorry."

"Natural reaction. It's hard to get prints off a narrow stem like that anyway."

McKernan bent over to sniff the glass. Not that he had any idea what bitter almonds smelled like. Mostly he smelled the alcohol and the sweetness of the wine.

"Where would the bottle of port be?"

"Down in the bar, I imagine. Teague the barman would know. It was Krieger's personal stock, so I doubt anyone else is going to be sampling it."

McKernan grunted. Importing anything from Earth was expensive. Most people drank locally distilled alcohol doctored with food coloring and flavoring to simulate the products of Earth. Being rich enough to drink imported wine after dinner every night belonged to a different world than his.

"I don't suppose there's any chance it could be suicide?"

"I doubt it," McAndrews said. "He didn't strike me as the sort that would take his own life. But I didn't really know him very well. Just as a member of the club."

"I thought you might have known him from Africa. That's where he's from, isn't it?"

"Africa is a big place, Erik. And long ago." There was something in McAndrew's tone that hinted at more, but the elder man didn't seem inclined to speak further.

"I must be getting too used to Mars," McKernan commented. "I forget sometimes that there's another world with billions of people."

"Mars is a small place in its own way," McAndrews replied. The population of Mars was a little over fifty thousand, with nearly half of that number living in and around Mars City.

"Just one other thing, and then I'll let you go."

"What is it, Erik?"

"Why didn't Krieger smell the cyanide? After all, he was in mining just like you, but obviously didn't notice it. Yet you spotted it right away."

"It's those damned cigars, I suppose. Ruins one's sense of smell. But I also think he'd had an accident when he was younger. A fire or something. Affected his nose and sinuses."

"Convenient," McKernan said to no one in particular. "I'll have to get forensics in here to take prints and pictures before we can move the body. I'll also need a list of who was in the club tonight, both staff and guests. I'll need to find out where everyone was during the evening, but that can wait until morning, I suppose. It's not like anyone is going anywhere."

"I can make a list for you. It's not that many people."

"Thanks, Otis. I know it's getting late, so I won't keep you any longer. Oh, when you go downstairs, tell the barman to put the port bottle where no one can get it, will you?"

"Of course."

After McAndrews had gone through the hatch to the stairs McKernan pulled out his communicator.

"Gaeretts? McKernan. Is Ferris handy?—Good. I need you to send him over to the Mars Club with the forensics kit. You'd better come along too. I've got a bunch of impatient executives on my hand and I'll want you to get statements from each of them as to their activities after dinner so we can let them go to their beds. We'll need a gurney for the body, too—.Yes, a body. It looks like there's been a murder at the Mars Club."

He descended the stairs to the main level of the club. He noted with satisfaction that Fenton had gathered all the members in the lounge. McAndrews was standing at the door, not quite guarding it, but there if anyone should attempt to leave.

"Gentlemen," McKernan said, there were no women in the Mars Club, "there has been an unfortunate incident. One of your number, Mr. Krieger, has died of what appears to be unnatural causes—"

"Unnatural causes? What's that suppose to mean?" The questioner was a chubby American by the name of Olberman. McKernan thought he was drunk.

"That's what we are trying to determine. Now, I'd appreciate it if you would all remain in this room until one of my men takes a statement from each of you as to your activities from the time dinner ended until now. He will be here shortly, so it shouldn't take long. Also, it would be best if you didn't try to compare stories before you make your statement. Otherwise, you are free to carry on as you wish. Thank you for your cooperation."

As he left to return to the Cupola, McKernan thought that his speech had gone well, considering that he'd been addressing what was probably the most powerful group of men on Mars.

CHAPTER 4
FERRIS VIEWS THE BODY

While he waited for Gaeretts, Ferris and the forensics kit, McKernan conducted a quick survey of the Cupola, exercising caution so as not to contaminate any possible evidence. There really wasn't much to see, at least that related to the case. It wasn't a particularly large room, and with the exception of a few seating groups scattered around, it was sparsely furnished. It was scrupulously clean with no signs of human occupancy except for the ashtray and the glass of port on the table next to the body. If someone had been up there with Krieger besides the butler, they hadn't left a trace.

Giving up the search as pointless; the inspector found himself staring out the dome into the Martian night. There wasn't much to see. Unlike Earth, the two moons of Mars were far too small to provide any illumination even if they had been above the horizon. The dim internal illumination of the dome obscured any stars. About all he could really make out were the lights of the spaceport off in the distance and those around the heavy industrial area in the opposite direction. It was actually quite a rare view. Most habitations on Mars were buried underground for protection from solar radiation. Even the windows of the buildings in Hut Town rarely gave views of anything except the adjacent huts.

McKernan was still gazing out into the darkness when Gaeretts and Ferris came through the hatch from below. The two were quite a contrast. Sergeant Gaeretts was a grizzled old Mars hand, the last of the men McKernan had inherited when he had first come up from Earth to take charge of the Trust Authority's police force. Before joining the security service Gaeretts had been a prospector and miner, a background that proved useful when dealing with the group which caused most of their problems, men in town for a few days to blow off steam. Gaeretts might not show much deference to his chief, but over the years since McKernan had come up to Mars, mutual respect and trust had built between the two men.

Ferris, on the other hand, was one of the youngest constables on the force, a gangling, baby faced kid who looked years younger than his actual age. Yet he'd been on Mars long enough for the planet to have put its mark on him. He'd taken on the lean, whipcord look of those who'd spent years on the red planet.

Addressing the older man, McKernan said, "There's a room full of people down in the lounge. I'll need statements from each of them as to their actions after dinner. Where they went, who they were with, etc. We need to establish some sort of timeline for everybody in the club between the time the dinner broke up until the time the body was discovered. Try to get as much information as possible, but don't drag it out. And Gaeretts—treat them as witnesses, not suspects. I don't want to antagonize anybody. As soon as you've gotten a statement from each of them, let them go to bed."

"I had to climb two flights of stairs for you to tell me that?" Gaeretts complained.

"You need the exercise. You'd have sneaked up to see the crime scene, anyway. Now climb back down the steps and get those statements before we have a VIP revolt on our hands." Gaeretts turned and went back through the airlock.

Turning to Ferris he asked, "Did you bring the forensics kit?" The Martian police force was far too small to have dedicated forensics technicians. As the nearest possibility for technical backup never came within fifty million kilometers, all the constables had been given at least some basic training in evidence gathering. Their capabilities were decades behind Earth standards, but they did the best they could.

In reply, Ferris held up the case they used to store the forensic equipment and set it down on one of the tables off to the side. Opening the case, he began to withdraw what he would need.

Ferris had been a raw kid when he had first come to Mars. Now he was into his second three year contract with the Trust Authority police force. His time on Mars had put an edge on him. He had learned to handle drunken miners in town for a spree with a maximum of efficiency and a minimum of risk. He could break up bar fights single-handed without calling for back up, which was just as well, because the police on Mars were stretched thin and constrained by the Trust Authority budget to a few dozen constables to cover a planet with a surface area equal to the land area of Earth.

But murder was rare on Mars, and the young constable looked on the body of Peter Krieger with a mixture of curiosity and apprehension. At least, McKernan thought, he didn't ask some inane question such as "Is that the body?" Instead his first words were "What do you want me to do, sir?" Despite his experiences over the last few years there was still a bit of hero worship on the part of the young constable for his superior.

"We'll need photos of the body, the table and anything else that catches your eye. Might as well shoot a video panning around the room as well just for the record. After that, check the table and the glass for prints. We'll need to save the contents of the glass for chemical testing, though it seems a pretty sure bet that it contains poison. Probably potassium cyanide. At least that's what it is according to McAndrews and he seems to know what he's talking about. After that, we'll have to get the body down from here and to the hospital for an autopsy. You brought a cart for the body?"

"Yes, sir. I left it outside in the concourse. I didn't know if you wanted it brought in here." *Here* being the Mars Club.

"Probably just as well. Wouldn't want to shock the members. Even though there's a good chance one of them is the murderer."

"You think so, sir?"

"You saw the security on the airlock downstairs. It has to have been a member or one of the staff."

"You're sure it was murder and not suicide?"

"The latter is a possibility, but unlikely, again according to McAndrews. Besides, this being Mars, I can think of easier ways to kill oneself than poison." They both knew that just turning off the life support for a surface suit was a quick and relatively painless route to death. "Well, I'll let you get on with the camera while I go down and question the butler. Oh, there will be a bottle of port that we'll have to take as evidence and get analyzed. It will probably be in the bar area."

Leaving Ferris to his work, McKernan descended to the main level. Waiting at the foot of the stairs was a man that McKernan recognized from his few previous visits to the club as the butler. He was a trim man of around fifty dressed in a dark suit and white shirt. He wasn't quite the image of a British butler as portrayed in fiction, but for Mars he was damned close.

"Mr. Fenton said that you might have a few questions for me, Chief Inspector." McKernan couldn't help smiling at the understatement. He'd had little enough to smile about lately.

"Yes, Jeeves," McKernan replied automatically. "You don't mind if I call you that, do you?"

"No, sir. I'm used to it. All the gentlemen do so. It's their little joke," he said without humor.

"You served Mr. Krieger the glass of port?"

"Yes, sir."

"And did you pour it yourself?"

"No, sir. That would have been Teague, the barman. He's is the one responsible for dispensing all alcoholic beverages, sir."

"I see," McKernan said. "Why don't you just take me through what happened from the time Mr. Krieger ordered the port until you discovered the body?"

"Of course, sir. After dinner, Mr. Krieger retired to the Cupola as was his custom. For port and a cigar. On his way out of the dining room he asked that I bring the port up to him. This was the usual thing, sir. I went into the bar and informed Teague. I then had several duties to perform, mostly having to do with clearing up after dinner. Once everyone had left the dining room I notified the kitchen of that fact I went around the club to see if anything else was needed. Most of the other gentlemen had retired to the lounge or the billiard room and several of them also had requests for drinks."

"So you didn't take the port straight up to the Cupola?"

"No , sir. I knew from past experience that Mr. Krieger would be in no hurry. He usually spent an hour or so up there after dinner. I went into the lounge to see what the gentlemen wanted and then into the billiard room as well for the same purpose. When I returned to the bar, Teague wasn't there, but the glass of port had been poured and was waiting on a tray. I took it up to Mr. Krieger. When I returned, Teague was back at the bar. I gave him the orders for the other drinks. I spent the next few minutes serving those drinks. It must have been a half hour or so later that I returned to the Cupola to see if there was anything more that I could do for Mr. Krieger, though he rarely had more than the one glass after dinner. That was when I discovered that he was dead. I immediately informed Mr. Fenton, the steward."

"How long was it from the time that you ordered the port until you found it waiting on the bar?"

"I can't say precisely, sir, as I did not note the time, but I'd estimate ten minutes or so. Certainly no more than fifteen."

"And did you notice any one in the bar during that time?"

"No, sir, but then I was either in the dining room, the lounge or the billiard room for most of that period."

"Thank you, Jeeves. I think that will be all for now. Do you know where I can find the barman?"

"I should think that he would be behind the bar, sir."

"Of course," McKernan said.

This proved to be the case. McKernan found James Teague, the barman, standing behind the bar polishing a glass with a white napkin. He was a short, slender man of African descent and was dressed in the short white jacket of his profession.

"What can I do for you, sir?" he asked in the accent of the Caribbean islands.

"I'm Inspector McKernan, and I'd like to ask you a few questions about tonight's incident, if I may?"

"I know who you are, sir" Teague replied. There was no particular animus behind the comment, just a certain amount of nervousness.

"I've already talked with the butler. He said that he gave you the order for a glass of port, and that when he came back for it, it was waiting on the bar, but that you were not present. Is that correct?"

"Yes, sir. I poured the port, and then I realized that I was getting low on Scotch. I knew that there would probably be several orders for it, so I went down to the storeroom to fetch another bottle. When I came back, the port was gone, so I assumed that Jeeves had taken it. Nothin' unusual in that, sir."

"Of course not. How long would you say you were away from the bar?"

"Oh, not long, sir. Maybe ten minutes. Maybe less. The storeroom is just down those stairs there," he said pointing to the a staircase that led downward off the corridor with the dining room. "I fetched the bottle of Scotch and another of vodka and came back up."

"Ten minutes seems a long time," McKernan commented.

"I had to open a new case for the vodka. That took a little time. I stacked the rest of the bottles from the case onto the shelf and then stacked the box with the other empties. Boxes are useful things, inspector, and people want them."

McKernan understood what the barman was saying. Nearly everything on Mars had to come from Earth. When no longer needed, items were repurposed as much as possible. Things were almost never just thrown away. Even an empty cardboard box had value. Teague continued, "I knew that the dinner had just broken up so that there was no rush."

"But during that period, the glass of port was unattended on the bar? There wasn't anyone else in the room?"

"No, sir, not when I left and not when I got back. After dinner most of the members had probably walked through into the lounge, but there wasn't anyone waiting in the bar."

"Do you have the bottle of port that you served from?"

"Yes, sir. It's right here." He turned to the back bar and unlocked a cabinet to one side from which he drew out a bottle. "This is it. Mr. Krieger's own private bottle."

"So it was not part of you general bar stock?"

"No, sir. Mr. Krieger had two cases shipped here for himself. Several of the gentlemen do that if they have a particular brand that they like. We charge a storage fee and a serving fee, too, but like I said, some of the gentlemen are particular."

"So no one else would have been served from this bottle?"

"Not unless Mr. Krieger told me to. He never did that, sir."

"Would anyone have access to this bottle besides you?"

"Mr. Fenton has a key to the cabinet, but no one else. I keep it locked, too, when I'm not on duty. I'd be responsible for any loss. And the liquor these gentlemen drink is pretty expensive."

"I can imagine."

"It wouldn't matter, though, inspector. No one tampered with that bottle. It was a fresh one. I opened it myself just before I poured the glass. Then I put the bottle back in the cabinet and locked it."

"Thanks, that's good to know. I'll have to take the bottle, though, to be tested. I'll sign a receipt, if you like."

"If you could, sir."

"Just so I have the timing straight, Jeeves came in with the Mr. Krieger's order and left. You got the bottle from the cabinet, opened it, poured the glass, and then put the bottle back into the cabinet. You then realized you needed more Scotch and left the bar to go to the store room downstairs. You were back in ten minutes or so, at which point the glass of port was gone, presumably carried by Jeeves up to Mr. Krieger in the Cupola."

"That just about sums it up, inspector."

"And during that time, to you knowledge, no one else was in the bar?"

"Like I said, there was no one here when I went down, and no one here when I came back up. More than that I can't say."

"Thank you. I don't think I have any other questions at the moment."

"Is there anything else I can do for you sir? A drink, perhaps?"

"Not at the moment, though I feel as if I could use one."

"So could I," Gaeretts said entering the bar. "I've got the statements and sent them all up to bed. Anything else for me to do?"

McKernan took the memory stick with the statements. "No, you can head back to the station. Ferris and I can take it from here."

CHAPTER 5
A SENSITIVE CASE

As McKernan was glancing at the notes Gaeretts had handed him on his comm, Ferris appeared coming down the stairway to the upper levels of the club.

"I've finished with the photos, sir," the constable said. "There wasn't much in the way of prints. I guess the body is ready to be moved."

"It's just you and me, constable. I sent the sergeant back to the station. Might as well get it over with," the inspector said with a shrug. "We can bring the gurney down the corridor here to the foot of the stairs. It's probably easier to carry the body down than to drag the cart up to the cupola."

With the force of gravity only a little over a third that on Earth, elevators were a rarity on Mars. Even the Mars Club was no exception. But even with the lower gravity McKernan knew from experience that moving a dead body was no easy chore. Krieger had been a big man who probably would have weighed close to a hundred kilos on Earth, the inspector thought ruefully.

He helped Ferris maneuver the gurney over the lip of the airlock at the entrance to the club. Thankfully, the members had all retired for the evening or left the club. They wouldn't have a crowd to observe and impede their efforts in getting the body down from the Cupola.

With the gurney positioned at the foot of the stairway, the two policemen ascended the steps without saying a word. As McKernan opened the hatch to the Cupola he noticed that there was a stop that could be used to keep it open. Part of him was appalled at such a breach of safety protocols while another part was thankful that they wouldn't have to deal with a self closing mechanism when they carried the body through.

The inspector got behind the body and got a grip underneath the armpits while Ferris grabbed the legs. McKernan knew the torso was the heavier portion, but he wouldn't be going down the steps backwards as they carried the body down. Fortunately, rigor mortis hadn't set in yet to add one more tribulation to their task.

The two of them managed to get Krieger down the steps and onto the gurney without any major difficulties. McKernan noted with approval that Ferris had made sure to bring along a sheet to cover the body. It was getting late, and there wouldn't be that many people around, but Ferris would have to wheel the cart through the Main Concourse to reach the hospital.

"Anything else, sir?" Ferris asked after they had gotten the gurney back out through the front airlock.

"There's a bottle of port in the bar that will need to be analyzed. That and the contents of the glass. Let the doctor know. That's about it. Might as well go home and get some sleep after you take care of that. We'll probably have a full day tomorrow conducting interviews. I'll let you know what our schedule is in the morning."

"Right, sir," Ferris said.   McKernan knew that the constable was pleased with the implication that he would be included in the investigation. Not that the inspector had much choice. Nearly half of his small force was spread out around the planet running patrols along what passed for roads on Mars or making occasional visits to the mining camps. That left him with less than a dozen constables to police what was in effect a small city with a population of over ten thousand individuals, nearly a fifth of the entire population of the planet.

McKernan saw him off, one wheel of the cart squeaking as it rolled over the concrete of the concourse towards the hospital, and then returned to the club. He wanted to secure the hatch to the Cupola and put it under seal so that no one disturbed the crime scene. After giving the room one last brief glance, he shut the hatch behind him and placed the seal. Descending the stairs, he was surprised to find Otis McAndrews waiting for him.

"You didn't have to wait up, sir. I think we've got things in hand."

"I've got that list you asked for. The people that were at dinner tonight. I've also included the names of all the staff."

"Thanks, that will be a big help. There wasn't any rush, though. Not much point in interviewing witnesses until the morning."

"Oh, it wasn't a big task. Do you have a moment, Erik?"

"Of course, sir. I'm done for the night. It's not as if any of the witnesses are going to leave town." That wasn't strictly true, of course. Someone might head out to the out there in a Mars buggy, though, with the help of observation satellites, McKernan wouldn't have much difficulty in tracking them down. But ships back to Earth were still relatively infrequent and watched closely. The next one wasn't scheduled to depart for nearly a week.

"Good. There are a few matters which we need to discuss." The older man gestured to a pair of chairs in the bar area. McKernan noticed that Teague had vanished.

"I took the liberty of ordering a pair of Scotches. I hope you don't mind?"

"I could use one, sir," McKernan said. Sitting down, he took a small sip of his drink. He knew that even before the cost of transporting it from Earth, it had been expensive, probably laid down in a cask in Speyside years before he had ever left Earth. It was a marked contrast from the grain alcohol adulterated with flavoring that made up most of what passed for whiskey on Mars.

McAndrews sat back in his chair, cradling his own drink in his hands, for a moment before asking:

"I don't suppose there's any chance that it *was* suicide?"

"I doubt it. Oh, the setting fits, of course. You could see someone going up there and quietly doing away with himself, but there are none of the other indicators. There was no note or anything like that. I'll have to investigate the possibility, of course, but I doubt it. You yourself said you didn't think he was the kind of man to kill himself."

"No he wasn't," McAndrews agreed. "It's unfortunate, though. A suicide would be much more convenient."

"Is there something you're not telling me, Otis?"

"I'm just cautioning you to tread carefully. This affair comes at a bad time. It needs to be handled quietly and with discretion."

"Why is that?" McKernan asked. He was puzzled. McAndrews knew that McKernan was well aware of the fact that in the club members he was dealing with the most powerful men on Mars. That went without say. So why the extra warning?

"There are reasons beyond the obvious as to why the matter has to be handled with more than the usual sensitivity. For example, one of the guests at dinner tonight was Louis Tsangambo."

"The Trust Authority Governor?"

"Yes. You may not be aware of the fact, but the governor, whoever he is, is always an honorary member of the club. Always has been since the founding of the club. As a matter of courtesy."

"You're not suggesting that the governor had anything to do with Krieger's death?"

"Lord, no. Don't even think that. I just wanted to point out the potential for political entanglements."

"Does the governor dine at the club often? I wouldn't think it was his sort of thing," McKernan asked. The Trust Authority governorship was a post given to men on their way up in the U.N. bureaucracy. They rarely stayed in the post more than a year before returning to a more comfortable position on Earth. None of the recent governors had been concerned with the improvement of conditions on Mars. Their major concern, other than avoiding any taint of scandal, was with maintaining the cut the U.N. made off of the mining concessions that were the whole reason for the settlement on Mars. As most of this money went to various projects in third-world countries, where it often served to line the pockets of the local politicians, the governors tended to be chosen for their political connections in those countries rather than any interest or ability in space exploration. The current holder of the post, Louis Tsangambo, was a former anti-colonial revolutionary whose opinions on the developed world were rarely concealed.

"No, not often. Maybe once a month. I think he keeps an eye on the menu and only comes when something particularly strikes his fancy. But I wish you'd forget about the governor. I'm quite sure he didn't do it. I just wanted to point out why this matter has to be handled in a sensitive manner."

McKernan could understand that. His relationship with the various governors had rarely been cordial. The constabulary was looked on as a barely necessary expense that cut into the budget of the Trust Authority, and any major crime that occurred could reflect badly on the sitting governor. That, and the fact that McKernan had personally been responsible for one holder of that post being forced into early retirement.

"Look, Erik, I'm going to tell you something in strictest confidence. Do I have your word that you won't reveal what I'm about to tell you?"

Given the number of confidences that McAndrews had shared with the inspector over the years, the mere act of asking the question served to indicate the import of what he was about to say.

"Of course, Otis. You have my word."

"Negotiations are currently going on with the United Nations about granting a certain degree of home rule for Mars. As you can imagine, these negotiations are extremely sensitive. If word were to get out, or if anything came to light that would show Mars in a bad light, it might jeopardize the discussions."

"Just who is doing the negotiating, and what do you mean by home rule?"

"Good questions, Erik. The negotiations are being driven by the mining companies with Anglo Martian taking the lead. As to what home rule would mean, that's also the subject of the discussions, but it would mean that the governor would become an elected position, and that some sort of local elected assembly would be able to pass laws and set budgets. At least within limits."

"So this is all being decided without any input from people on Mars?" Erik asked skeptically.

"That's the political reality, Erik. People on Mars don't have any sort of political leverage back on Earth."

"Just why are the companies so interested in promoting home rule? I would think that would be the last thing they'd want."

"Think about it, Erik. The Trust Authority and the companies have been increasingly at loggerheads. All the Trust Authority cares about is to milk Mars for as much as they can get in the short term. They don't care about development or the welfare of the people on Mars. They particularly aren't thinking about the future."

"And the companies do?"

"It's good for business. Let's face it, at least half of the people on Mars work directly for one or the other of the companies. Most of the rest, except for those employed directly by the Trust Authority, depend on the companies in one way or another for their lively hood. I think you'll find that the interests of the companies and those of the people on Mars coincide more often than you think."

"We've heard this all before, Otis. After the United Semi fiasco things were supposed to change. You were appointed temporary governor. And it all came to naught when the U.N. reneged."

"That's why these negotiations are so sensitive. There are a lot of people in the U.N. who don't want to see any sort of home rule for Mars. They want to keep it as a colony whose only purpose is to provide resources for Earth."

"Don't you think that a bit ironic, given that most of those same people complain about the colonial exploitation their countries suffered in the past?"

"We both know that those complaints have been mainly to promote political agendas. And that is why the companies are so interested in wresting control from the Trust Authority even if it does mean ceding it to the people of Mars. At least the people on Mars have a vested interest in developing the planet."

"I'll believe it when I see it, Otis. But I'll keep my investigation as discrete as I can. It will go where the evidence leads it."

"That's all that I can ask, Erik."

CHAPTER 6
BEDTIME STORIES

McKernan walked the Secretary to the airlock. McAndrews, unlike many of the club's members, kept a separate residence suite in the office space occupied by Anglo-Martian. After seeing him out through the door, the inspector took a quick stroll through the club. He'd been inside several times before, but had never had the opportunity to really familiarize himself with the layout. He had a feeling that understanding the lay of the land might prove important.

The airlock opened out into a reception area or vestibule. This contained several small seating groups and a high desk, behind which was a door leading to the office of Fenton, the club steward. Two corridors, one on either side, led towards the rear of the club from this front area. Off the one on the left was the billiard room, lounge, and a rest room. In the middle, behind Fenton's office, was the bar area which consisted of the bar proper backing onto the steward's office and several tables and sofas. Beyond this were the stairs leading up to the members' suites and down to the kitchen and storerooms. A narrower hallway ran from side to side at the rear of the club. McKernan knew from experience that off of this were several smaller rooms used for private meetings or dining. Coming back up the other corridor were the dining room and library, the latter equipped with tables, computers and communications equipment as well as a number of video display screens with news feeds and the latest results from the various exchanges on Earth. As he walked up the corridor, McKernan noted that the most convenient path between the dining room and either the lounge or the billiard room passed through the bar area.

It struck McKernan that the Mars Club, whatever power and wealth it might represent, was not a particularly large establishment. There were few places to hide and even fewer ways to avoid being observed by the other members. Yet someone had managed to slip a deadly poison into a glass of port standing in plain view on the bar. And it fell on his shoulders to determine who. But not that night, the inspector decided. There was little more that he could do at the moment. The witnesses were for the most part already in their beds. There wasn't much point in dragging them out to ask a few questions when they could just as easily be asked in the morning. It was not as if anyone was going anywhere. For that matter, he could use some sleep himself.

It was already past midnight. The lights had been turned down, and except for Jeeves and Teague who were collecting the glassware, the main floor of the club was empty. Somehow, in the dim light it seemed much smaller and more hollow than it had under full illumination.

McKernan gave a shrug.

He made his way through the air-tight doors of the front lock and out into the Concourse. The lights had been turned down there as well. Power was still a limited commodity on Mars, particularly at night when the solar arrays weren't on line, and every effort was made to conserve electricity wherever possible.

Only a few people were still to be seen on the concourse, either making their way home or on some work related task. Except for some of the wilder sections of Hut Town, Martians tended to go to bed early.

Without giving it any thought, McKernan took the hallway off the concourse that led to Corridor B. A short walk later he was at the airlock that marked the border between Mars City proper and Hut Town. Automatically, he worked the controls of the lock and stepped through.

Suddenly he was in another world. Gone were the hard, antiseptically clean surfaces of fused silica blocks and tile. In their place was a metal grate floor and the curved sides of the cylinder that formed the corridor. The conduits that fed the widely spaced overhead lights were exposed and hanging from the ceiling. The corridor was a remnant of the original settlement, a thin walled tube that had been inflated and then sprayed from the inside with a coat of insulating foam.

At irregular intervals, airlocks had been let into the sides of the tunnel. This close to Mars City, most led into commercial enterprises of one sort or another, shops, offices of small companies, some light manufacturing and repair facilities. Farther out along the corridor were the residences of those who either couldn't afford to or chose not to live in the company dorms in the city. At the far end of the corridors were the bars, flop houses, and bordellos that catered to miners and construction works in town for a spree, though Corridor B was a little too genteel to have much of that.

There was no one in sight. Few people chose to linger in the corridors of Hut Town even during the day. Even though this length of corridor had been buried, the temperature was a good ten degrees colder than it had been in Mars City. Farther out, where the corridor was still above grade, the temperature would be even colder. No sense in heating unused space. Nor was anything but the necessary maintenance performed. The ever present red Martian dust tended to collect in the corners and nooks.

This was the world that McKernan had called home for the last six years.

He passed through another lock into a nearly identical length of corridor, and then through a third before stopping in front of the airlock that served as the entrance to his own hut.   He noted with satisfaction that Elizabeth had remembered to lock it. He punched in the entry code and passed through the airlock.

Inside, the hut was in darkness except for the glow from the readouts on the life support panel. Elisabeth had gone to bed. He hadn't really expected her to wait up. After all, she had an early shift at the hospital in the morning.

Trying to make as little noise as possible, he went into the bedroom. Undressing, he piled his clothes on the chair next to his side of the bed. The pistol and his communicator were placed on top of the night stand.

The sheets were cold against his skin, but he could sense the warmth of the body on the other side of the bed. As he lay on his side he could feel her shift closer to him, feel her arm as she draped it around his body.

"Was there trouble?" she asked, in a sleepy voice.

"Nothing serious. Just a murder at the Mars Club."

"A murder?" Elisabeth was suddenly alert. "At the Mars Club? Who? How?"

"One of the members. He was poisoned. Apparently cyanide in his port."

"Are you joking Erik?"

"I only wish I were," McKernan responded. "This could turn out to be a big mess."

"Who was it? Anyone I'd know?"

"I doubt it. His name was Peter Krieger. He was the head of Pretoria Mining."

"Do you know who did it?"

"I haven't a clue. As far as I can tell, it might have been anyone in the club tonight. And that includes the governor."

"You *are* joking about that. Aren't you?"

"He was there."

"But he's not really a suspect—Is he?"

"Along with a dozen or so of the most powerful men on Mars."

"I still can't believe it." The doctor tried to stifle a giggle. It had been some time since McKernan had heard her laugh. "It sounds like one of those old British mysteries. Chief Inspector McKernan and the Case of the Poisoned Port."

"Go to sleep," McKernan answered, rolling over to face her. Eventually they did.

CHAPTER 7
TOO MANY SUSPECTS

McKernan woke to the smell of coffee. He could hear Elisabeth in the kitchen in the other section of the hut. A quick glance at his communicator told him it was 0750. He had slept later than he had planned, but then it had been a late night.

Elisabeth popped her head into the bedroom. She was wearing her hospital scrubs, her blonde hair pulled back in a pony tail.

"I've got to run, Erik. I'm due at the hospital at 0800. There's hot coffee in the pot." She turned to go, then called back, "Will you be home for dinner tonight?"

"Probably. Unless something breaks on this case, which I don't expect."

"OK. I'll see you then," she said as she went back through the lock joining the two sections of the hut. McKernan could hear the sound of the front lock opening as she left. For a moment after he had come in the previous night the old magic had been there, but now the tenseness that had characterized their relationship the last few months had returned. They both knew that the clock was ticking, and if Elisabeth didn't sign a new contract soon she'd be heading back to Earth and their relationship would be over.

Erik pulled on his jeans and a sweater and crossed over into the kitchen. It was warmer there. Since Elisabeth had moved in he had kept the heater turned up a few degrees.

He'd made quite a few adjustments over the last year and a half.

He made himself a quick scramble of eggs, peppers and onions. Fresh vegetables were relatively plentiful on Mars, particularly if you grew them yourself.   Fruits were a different matter. One of things that he missed was orange juice, which, because it had to be shipped from Earth, was expensive and rare. Coffee was expensive, too, but it could be reduced to a super desiccated form that, while lacking somewhat in flavor, was at least affordable. He poured himself a cup of coffee and sat down at the table with the list McAndrews had given him the previous night.

In typical fashion, Otis had put his own name at the top of the list. That was fair enough. At the moment he was as much a suspect as anyone else at the club.

The next name was Louis Tsangambo, the Trust Authority Governor. He'd only been on Mars for about six months, and probably would be back on Earth in less time than that. Governors tended to not last long. At best, they were political appointees using Mars as a stepping stone in their career plans. The worst had been a corrupt fool who had tried to line his own pockets at the expense of everyone else. Fortunately, latest holder of the office had proved to be a hands off kind of manager who Erik hadn't had to deal much with.

He knew that the governor wasn't liked by the mining companies. Given his background, that wasn't surprising. Tsangambo was a died in the wool people's revolutionary, a product of the interminable unrest that had plagued Africa since the twentieth century.   As such, he was more interested in refighting the anti-colonial wars of that era than finding solutions that worked to everyone's advantage.

Was he a likely murder suspect? Possibly. The victim had been a white South African who embodied all that

Tsangambo was against. But whatever antipathy he had had for Krieger was impersonal as far as the inspector was aware. Murder, particularly poisoning, implied a more intimate relationship than the two had had.

For the moment, McKernan considered it unlikely that the governor was the murderer and he continued to work his way down the list. The next two names were those of Boris Kasperovski, of the Siberian Mining Conglomerate and Wu "Charlie" Lin of the People's Celestial Minerals Corporation. Both Siberian and Celestial were technically quasi-state enterprises, but their two heads were both more corporate bureaucrat than politician. McKernan didn't know that much about either one except for the fact that they were rivals. If they were going to murder anyone, it was would have been more likely to have been each other than Krieger.

Kenji Fujika was the next name on the list, manager of Fukashima Rare Earths. McKernan knew him better than most of the others. Fujika had spent part of his time growing up in the U.S. where his father had managed operations for a Japanese company. He had gone to college at UCLA and spoke perfect, unaccented southern California English. He was likeable, an amusing conversationalist, and an avid follower of American football. He showed up often when replays of games were on the screen at Finnegan's. He didn't seem a likely murder suspect, either.

Francois DuChene was the head of European Space Ventures. The few times McKernan had met him he had seemed the typical arrogant Frenchman. That, however, the inspector realized wasn't enough to make him a prime suspect.

Helmut Nordlund was next on the list. He was the head of local operations for Interplanetary Transport, the corporation that flew the spaceships that provided Mars' lifeline to Earth. Technically, he was probably a lower level functionary than the others on the list, but as the man responsible for getting things to and from Mars he was someone whose good side you wanted to keep on. Fortunately, Helmut was a cosmopolitan Dane who spoke everyone's language and never seemed to take things personally.   Not much of a suspect, either McKernan thought to himself.

Three others, the inspector couldn't remember ever having met.   They were Leo Kichler who was the representative of Rio Plata Mining, an Argentine of German descent, Robert Gordon, a Canadian who worked for Northern & Big Sky Mining and who had just arrived on Mars in the last month, and Stan Olberman, an American who was the head of Transamerican Minerals.

So much for the members.   Unless there was some hidden link, none of them would seem to be a likely candidate for the poisoner.

McAndrews had also listed the staff. McKernan didn't really know any of them, which wasn't surprising. They probably kept to the Mars Club most of the time.   In addition to Fenton, the steward, Watson the butler, and Teague the bartender, there was also Jose Duro, the chef, his assistant, Alphonso Allicante, a Mrs. Alice Simpson, the housekeeper, and Walter Duckworth who acted as janitor and maintenance man. He'd have to check their files when he had the chance, but on the surface he had trouble imagining a link between any of them and Krieger.

As he was cleaning up the dishes before leaving his communicator sounded. It was Dr. Greenwood from the hospital.   Greenwood was near the end of his second contract which was unusual for the medical staff, most of whom turned over at the expiration of their first.   He showed every sign of becoming a permanent Martian. He could be testy and abrupt, but he was also the most respected medical man on the planet if not the most liked.

"I've got some preliminary findings for you, McKernan," he said when the inspector answered.

"So, was he poisoned?"

"Either McAndrews knows his stuff or he got lucky. Cause of death, potassium cyanide poisoning. Not much question about it."

"Was it in the port?"

"The contents of the glass contained enough to have killed half a dozen people. The bottle was clean. No evidence that it had been tampered with."

"How quickly would the cyanide have acted?'

"Almost immediately. Fifteen seconds or less would be my guess."

"Thanks, doc."

"Anything else?"

"How easy would it be to find potassium cyanide on Mars?"

"Pretty easy for anyone with access to a chemical supply room. We've got a kilo of the stuff in the lab here at the hospital. I imagine that most of the mining company labs have gallons of it laying around. Machine shops, too. The stuff is used in a lot of industrial processes."

"Any idea in what form it was introduced into the port?"

"I don't have any evidence, but if I had to make a guess, I'd say in crystal or powdered form. That would be the easiest to handle. Say half a teaspoon. The crystal form looks a lot like table salt."

"Thanks, doc. I'll let you know if I have any more questions."

Greenwood hung up without saying good-bye.

So, McKernan thought, that simplified things. The poison was in the glass but not in the bottle. Sometime in the five or ten minutes that the glass had sat on the bar someone had walked by, dumped a half teaspoon of cyanide in the glass and walked away. That is unless Teague had poisoned the port when he had poured it. Or Watson had poisoned it before delivering it to Krieger in the Cupola.

Well, he wasn't going to solve this case with speculation, McKernan concluded. It was time to get to work.

CHAPTER 8
NO SKELETONS IN THE CELLAR

McKernan had arranged to meet Ferris at the Mars Club. The constable was waiting for him just outside the entrance. He had an eager look on his face and a handful of papers in his hand. While he had been involved peripherally in a number of homicide cases before, this would be the first time he was part of the investigation.

"Ready to go, Ferris?" McKernan asked.

"Yes, sir," the constable replied. Holding out the papers he added, "I typed up the notes of Sergeant Gaeretts interviews last night."

"Good work, but that could have waited for Gaeretts to do it."

"You know how the sergeant is with paperwork," Ferris said with a smile.

"Well, let's see if they're awake inside," McKernan said as he pushed the button below the sign.

Fenton was waiting in the vestibule for them when they had passed through the airlock. The steward, though still impeccably groomed, seemed more nervous than he had the previous evening, glancing about continuously in quick furtive motions. In a way, McKernan could understand the man's unease. He was being paid, probably quite handsomely, to ensure the smooth running of the operation that was the Mars Club. A police investigation, especially one for murder, where the prime suspects were the members and staff of that entity, was certain to be disruptive.

McKernan's first words on entering the club did nothing to dispel Fenton's concerns: "I will need to interview all those present at the dinner last night. That will include all of the staff." Understanding the standing of those who had attended the dinner, he specifically avoided the term interrogate.

"I see—" Fenton responded. "Am I to understand that this means you believe that Mr. Krieger's death was neither a suicide or an accident?"

"We are investigating all possibilities, of course, but unless you keep potassium cyanide lying around in the salt shakers or the sugar bowl, I think an accident can be ruled out. We've found none of the usual signs that usually accompany a suicide, either, such as a note."

"I see—. Well, I am afraid that at the moment most of the members are not on the premises. Most of the gentlemen are in fact early risers and have already left for their offices."

"I understand. I wasn't actually expecting to be able to interview them immediately. However, I was hoping that you would be able to provide a space here at the club where we could work and conduct our interviews. I know they are busy men, and I would prefer not to inconvenience any of them by hauling them down to the police station," McKernan said dryly.

The steward blanched at the thought. "I'm sure the gentlemen will appreciate your consideration, inspector. As you are aware, there are several private dining rooms in the club. I can offer the use of one of those during the course of your investigations."

"Yes, I think that would be quite helpful. Thank you. Also, I understand that the club has a lower level that houses the kitchens and storerooms. Would it be possible for you to provide us with a quick tour?"

"Certainly, inspector. If you will follow me?" Fenton looked relieved to be able to escort McKernan and the constable out of the vestibule.

They walked down the corridor on the lounge side of the club towards the rear of the building, passing the bar area to arrive at the steps leading down towards the cellar. McKernan noted the door of the restroom opposite the steps. The stairway leading to the upper levels was accessed from the other corridor which ran past the dining room so that the two sets of steps were stacked one above the other.

As they followed Fenton down the steps McKernan asked, "Is this the only way to the kitchens and storerooms?"

"Yes, there's just the one set of stairs," the steward answered.

"And the food is brought up these steps? That seems rather inconvenient."

Looking back up the stairs towards the inspector, Fenton replied, "Oh, well, yes, there is a dumb waiter from the kitchens to the butler's pantry adjacent to the dining room, but it's not really meant for people to use. Just carts to carry the trays of food and bring the dirty dishes down. It's not even a meter square. I'll show it to you when we get to the kitchen."

As they descended the steps the paneling of the main floor of the club gave way to white tile walls and stainless steel fixtures, somewhat institutional in appearance, but not that different than many commercial kitchens back on Earth.

"As you can see, this is the kitchen space," the steward indicated with a gesture of his hand as they reached the cellar. The stairway gave out directly into the kitchen with no intervening door. McKernan could see the usual arrangement of prep tables, ovens, and cook tops, all of course using electricity rather than gas. It was, in reality, a very compact space, laid out with efficiency and the small staff in mind and kept remarkably neat and tidy. It reminded McKernan of nothing so much as the galley of the naval ship he had once been posted to during his service days back on Earth.

The inspector looked around curiously, noting the positions of the various task areas in relation to the staircase.

"So, anyone coming down those stairs would be visible to those working in the kitchen?" McKernan mused, half to themselves.

"Yes, I suppose so," Fenton replied, "depending on where they were working or if they bothered to look up."

"Of course," McKernan answered in return.

"Is that important?"

"Maybe. Teague said he came down here to fetch a couple of bottles for the bar. It seems likely that the poison was introduced into the glass of port during the interval he was away from the bar. That is presupposing that he didn't poison the port himself. Or that Jeeves isn't the culprit."

"Yes—," Fenton said rather awkwardly.

"Just where is the store room?"

"The wine and spirits are kept down here," Fenton said, pointing down a short hall that lead away from the kitchen.

The door to the wine storage area proved to be a stout metal affair with a lock accessed using an electronic key card.

"Rather impressive security," McKernan commented wryly.

"Well, there is quite a lot of expensive merchandise in here," Fenton explained.

"I don't suppose it would be possible for me to peek inside?"

"Any particular reason, inspector?"

"Let's just say I'm curious? I appreciate a good bottle of wine as much as the next man."

The steward shrugged, produced a key card from his vest pocket and opened the door. A light came on automatically. He invited the inspector in with a wave of his hand. After the two of them had entered, the door swung closed behind them. It was quite chilly inside, but then that was to be expected.

"The door closes automatically?" McKernan said in surprise.

"As I said, the contents are quite valuable. It was felt necessary to have the door close on its own to prevent it from being left open through negligence."

McKernan only half heard the steward's answer as he gazed around the room in envy. One wall was given over to wine, either in bottles or cases, all neatly labeled with the names of some of the best vineyards of Europe, America, Chile and Australia. There was a separate cooler for the white wines. The other wall held cases of Scotch, bourbon, vodka and other spirits, all with labels that would have qualified them as "top shelf" back on Earth.

Interestingly, the far end of the room was given over to a collection of small lockers, each with its own lock. Behind the mesh of the locker doors McKernan could see various bottles laid down neatly.

To McKernan's enquiring look Fenton replied, "Some of the members have their own private stores of special bottles."

"Including Mr. Krieger?"

"Yes, I believe so," the steward answered. Peering at the labels on the lockers he pointed one out. "Here it is, right here." Looking through the door McKernan could see a half dozen bottles, all with the same label as on the bottle of port he had seen the night before.

"All very interesting, but probably not relevant."

"Inspector?" the steward queried in puzzlement.

"We've established that the bottle of port Mr. Krieger drank from last night had not been tampered with, so there is no reason to assume any foul play occurred down here. I was mostly concerned with whether Teague, when he was down here, would be aware of anyone creeping up the stairs to sabotage the glass sitting on the bar. But with the thickness of these walls and the door shut that seems unlikely. I think I've seen enough here. You mentioned a dumb waiter up to the dining room?"

"Right this way," Fenton said opening the door to the wine storage room. McKernan noted that from the inside the door was opened by a simple handle with no security card required.

As Fenton had explained earlier, the dumb waiter proved to be a small affair located at one end of the kitchen conveniently next to the washing up area. The elevator, itself, was about a meter deep, slightly less wide, and just over a meter high, just large enough to accommodate one of the serving carts employed in the kitchen. It would be possible for a man to ride in the car, though it would not be particularly comfortable. The whole was operated by two buttons labeled prosaically "UP" and "DOWN." As the car was currently on the kitchen level, McKernan experimentally pressed the "UP" button.

The car began to ascend at a not particularly spectacular pace. More importantly, an electronic tone began to sound, not really obtrusive, but not easily ignored.

"Well, I think we can rule out the use of the dumb waiter. At least not unless the entire kitchen staff was involved. Speaking of which, how many are on the staff."

"There are really just the two, Chef Duro and his assistant Alphonso Allicante. We rarely need to serve more than a dozen people at a time, and that is more than sufficient. We can bring in temporary help if needed."

"And do they normally remain down here during meals?"

"Yes, normally. Jeeves takes care of the serving, though occasionally I will assist with the wine or coffee. Of course, before and during the actual meal the two chefs are busy, and afterwards they do cleaning up."

"But one or the other of them could absent himself for a minute or two?"

"I couldn't say," Fenton answered noncommittally.

Shifting the topic, McKernan asked, "How do you bring in supplies? Not through the front door I would expect?"

"No. There is a service hatch on this level. As you are undoubtedly aware the whole city has a lower level of tunnels for utilities and deliveries."

McKernan was in fact aware of the existence of these tunnels though surprisingly many of the city's residents were not.

"Could I see it, please?"

"Of course. It's down at this end of the kitchen."

The door proved unremarkable, being a standard air-tight pressure hatch. This one was equipped with a mechanical lock and pressure tell-tales to indicate the state of the tunnel on the other side.

"Is this hatch monitored electronically?"

"Yes it is," Fenton answered.

"I'd like to know if it was opened at all yesterday."

"Just a moment, inspector," Fenton said, reaching for his communicator. A quick flicker of his fingers brought up the desired data. He showed McKernan the screen. "As you can see, inspector, the hatch hasn't been opened for several days. It's usually only opened when we receive supplies or remove the trash."

"Well, we can rule out ninja assassins sneaking in, then," Mckernan said, unable to restrain himself. "Is there anything else down here?"

"The staff quarters are at the front of the building."

"All of the staff live at the club?"

"Yes.   It's   actually   one   of   the   perks.   The accommodations are quite pleasant if not overly large."

McKernan could see the attraction. The housing provided by the Trust Authority and the various corporations tended to make the average college dorm room look palatial by comparison.

"We might as well look at them while we're down here," McKernan said, though he doubted that they would have any relevance to the investigation.

As promised, the staff quarters were pleasant if compact. In addition to individual rooms, there was a commons area with a dining table, sofa and lounge chairs, an exercise room and bathing and laundry facilities.

"In addition to myself, there are six on staff at the moment, though there are quarters for eight. This one is vacant at the moment, but is fairly typical. Mine, of course, is somewhat larger," Fenton explained smugly as he opened a door to show McKernan one of the rooms.

It was about four meters by three and furnished with a bed, a comfortable looking chair, desk space and a storage unit. A sink and toilet stood at one end. The walls were painted a rather attractive shade of blue and the concrete of the floor was covered with an area rug. There were, of course, no windows, but that wasn't unusual for Mars City.

"I think we've seen enough down here for the moment, Mr. Fenton. Thank you for your cooperation. I'll want to interview each of the staff as convenient."

"Anything I can do to help, inspector. I'll be happy to get this matter resolved as quickly as possible."

"As will I," McKernan agreed. "Which room did you say I could use?"

"Will the one in the left rear corner do? There is a table and several chairs in there now as well as a white board."

"That should do just fine," McKernan assured him.

CHAPTER 9
MR. FUJIKA GIVES EVIDENCE

As they came up the stairs from the kitchens McKernan spotted Kenji Fujika in the corridor. Taller than the average Japanese, Fujika was a trim, athletic looking man in his late forties. Like McKernan, he was dressed casually in jeans and a sweater, and had a computer tablet in a bag slung over his shoulder.

"Do you have a moment, sir?" McKernan said as he approached the executive.

"Good morning, Inspector. It's about Krieger I assume?"

"Yes. I'd like to ask you a few questions about where you were after dinner last night. Purely a formality. I'll be interviewing everyone who was in attendance last night."

"Of course." Fujika took a quick look at his watch. "I've got a meeting in twenty minutes, but I can spare you time until then."

"Thank you. That should be more than enough time. If you'll come this way, the Club has made a room available to me where we won't be interrupted."

He led the executive to the private dining rooms at the rear of the club that Fenton had allocated them. Located as it was out of the way in the far back corner it suited McKernan just fine.

The inspector offered Fujika a seat and then took the one opposite, placing his communicator on the table. Ferris, not quite sure what to do, sat in a chair off to the side.

"Just so you know, sir, I will be recording this conversation."

"Of course," Fujika said with a hint of a smile. "Just like in a detective video."

"Yes sir, just like in a video," McKernan replied. "I have a list of those who were at dinner last night, but not where people were sitting. Perhaps we could start with that."

"OK. Well, you have to understand that it was a Friday night. Most nights, people just come whenever and sit either alone or with whomever they want. But Friday nights are a bit more formal. It's something of a tradition. We all sit down at one big table at 1930 after cocktails. We're supposed to notify Fenton if we're going to attend and he arranges the seating order. That is mostly to avoid conflicts."

"Are there many of those?"

"Not really. Of course some people get on better than others, but I'm not aware of any real problems. We're all men of business. Anyway. Otis as Secretary normally sits at the head of the table, but as the Governor was in attendance, he took the place of honor and Otis sat at the foot. Let's see, if I can remember the rest. Wu Lin sat at the Governor's right, followed by Leo Kichler, Robert Gordon, Francois DuChene, and Boris Kasperovski. I sat on his left followed by Krieger and Stan Olberman and Helmut Nordlund."

"And about how long did the meal take?"

"Oh, about an hour and a half. Friday dinners tend to be pretty leisurely. Coffee was served a little before 2100 I think."

"And what happened after dinner?"

"Well, Wu Lin, Stan, Francois and I had made arrangements to play some bridge, so we wandered into the lounge. I think Leo and Robert went into the billiards room for a game. Krieger, of course headed up to the Cupola. Otis and Helmut came into the lounge as well. I think Boris went to the library to work on some correspondence. Oh, and the Governor had a few words with Fenton and then left. He doesn't really like to associate with us capitalists."

"So everybody left the dining room at once and headed for the lounge or the billiard room? They didn't say go up to their rooms or the bar or anywhere else?"

"Well, it's not like we all got up and rushed out en masse. I think Krieger got up first. He was never much for socializing. We all had to go through the motions of thanking the Governor for gracing us with his presence. And of course after sitting at the table for nearly two hours and drinking some really decent wine most of us slipped away to the loo. I know I did."

"That's right by the bar, isn't it?"

"Yes. Convenient."

"I don't suppose you noticed who went when?"

"Sorry. Not really. I do remember that Otis was coming out as I went in, if that helps. I think Stan came in just after me."

"You don't happen to remember if there was a glass of port sitting on the bar at the time, do you?" the inspector queried.

"Now that you mention it, yes I think I do. But I don't remember seeing Teague."

"I think he had to fetch something from the cellar," McKernan supplied.

Fujika looked thoughtful for a moment.

"Am I to take it from your line of questioning, Inspector, that you aren't altogether convinced that Krieger's death was a suicide?"

McKernan looked at the executive, wondering just how much he should confide in him. There didn't seem to be much point in concealing the fact that it had been murder.

"We are looking into the possibility that cyanide was slipped into the glass of port as it sat on the bar."

"Cyanide? But that would imply that you suspect one of the members of murder, wouldn't it."

McKernan tried to read the other's expression, but all he could detected was surprise.

"Yes, I'm afraid so. Or one of the staff."

"This *is* starting to sound like a mystery show. 'The Poisoned Port Case.' And I presume that we are all suspects," Fujika commented, almost as if he was enjoying the fact.

"For the moment, until I have evidence to the contrary," McKernan replied pleasantly. "Just how well did you know Mr. Krieger?"

"Not well at all, I'm afraid. Which is strange, when you think about it. I know most of the members fairly well. After all, there isn't that much to do on Mars, so you get to talking about yourself. Especially after a few drinks. But Krieger wasn't a very friendly guy. Kept mostly to himself. Never spoke about his past. And of course he didn't like anyone he thought of as *kafirs*."

"Excuse me?"

"He didn't like anyone who wasn't white. Like Wu Lin or myself. Or the Governor. He hated Tsangambo with a passion. I think the feeling was mutual as far as the Governor went."

"Was the feeling strong enough to lead to murder?"

"Not that I know of. Frankly, I don't know either of them well enough to really say one way or the other. Mostly, they made a point of ignoring each other. I think that's one of the reasons Kreiger headed up to the Cupola right after dinner, so he wouldn't have to speak with Tsangambo. He got up from the table, talked to Jeeves, probably to order his port, and then left the dining room."

"Do you know how Krieger got on with the staff? Did he have any problems with them? Teague for instance?"

"Not that I know of. He wasn't chummy with any of them, but he was never purposely rude, either. Mostly indifferent. As far as Teague goes, I never saw any animosity. I think he thought it was all right for a black man to be a servant. He just didn't consider them his equals."

"What about the other members? Do you know of any problems between any of them and Krieger?"

Fujika was silent for a moment as if he was weighing just how much he should say.

"No, can't say that I do. Of course, most of us except for Helmut and Francois are in competition with each other, but Mars is a big place and there are plenty of opportunities for us all. I'm not aware of any real conflict. Certainly nothing that would lead to murder."

Fujika looked at his watch.

"I do have a meeting in a few minutes, Inspector."

"Of course, sir. I think you've answered all my questions for the moment. You've been quite helpful. I'll let you go."

"I suppose this is the point where you tell me not to leave town?" Fujika quipped.

"Oh, I don't think that will be necessary," McKernan replied.

"If you have any other questions, Inspector, you can leave word with Fenton or contact my office."

"I'll keep that in mind, sir," McKernan said as he stood and shook the other's hand. After Fujika had left, the inspector wondered to himself if that was one person he could strike off his list of suspects, or had the executive's affability and helpfulness been just a cover?

CHAPTER 10
COMINGS AND GOINGS

"So what do you think of Mr. Fujika's statement, constable?" McKernan asked when he had left.

"He didn't seem to me like someone with anything to hide, sir."

"No he didn't, did he. Either he's not our murderer, or he's a very clever liar. You did notice that he didn't tell us anything that we wouldn't find out anyway."

"Do you really suspect him, sir?"

"No, not really. I think Mr. Fujika is exactly what he seems, an innocent bystander who finds this whole mess an entertaining break from the routine."

"So what do we do now, sir?" Ferris asked.

"I think that what we need to do before we start interviewing any more people is to get things straight in our own minds so we know what questions to ask. When I questioned Teague last night he said that he had had to make a trip to the storeroom in the cellar and left the bar untended for what may have been as long as ten minutes with the glass of port sitting on the bar. If we rule out Teague or the butler as our poisoner, it's most likely that the murderer acted while Teague was gone. It seems to me that what we need to do is to determine who had the opportunity to dump the cyanide into the port while it was sitting on the bar."

"Ten minutes is a long time, sir."

"Yes, it is. When we interviewed Kenji Fujika just now, he said that things didn't break up all at once after dinner, but that people hung around for a bit and then left, more or less one at a time. What we have to do is see if we can come up with a timeline of their movements. Maybe that will point us in the right direction."

"But how can we do that?"

"We can start by sorting through the statements Gaeretts took last night. I suggest that we both spend a few minutes reading them over."

The statements for the most part had been short and not terribly informative. Ferris, perhaps trying too hard, was taking his time reading over the notes in an effort to be thorough. The inspector, for his part, had finished first and began to sketch a rough floor plan of the club using the white board and markers with which the room had conveniently come equipped.

"OK. This is the club," McKernan said, pointing at the sketch. "Here's the dining room. Now from the statements we know that Fujika, Wu, Olberman and DuChene ended up in the lounge playing bridge. Kichler and Gordon went to played billiards. Nordlund and McAndrews also went to the lounge to read. Kasperovski went to work on correspondence in the library. The governor left the club after talking to various people after dinner. Did I miss anyone?"

"What about Fenton and the butler?" Ferris replied.

"Jeeves was moving around quite a bit. He was in and out of the dining room and eventually went to the lounge, billiard room and library gathering drink orders. As to Fenton, well I'm not sure. We can ask him later."

McKernan stared at the board for a moment. "One thing we know is that several of the members went to the restroom here," pointing at the location on his plan. "Presumably, not all at once. Let's see—" he said paging through the notes on his computer tablet. "McAndrews,

Fujika, Olberman, Wu Lin, Kichler, and Nordlund. Now from what Fujika said, McAndrews was coming out as he was going in, and Olberman entered while he was still in the restroom."

The inspector wrote down the names on the board in that order. "Now what about the other three?"

"Is it important, sir" the constable asked.

"Who knows?" McKernan responded with a shrug.

"Well, Mr. Wu Lin must have come after Mr. Kichler, because he says he saw him walking towards the billiard room."

"And Nordlund?"

"He doesn't say who was before or after him. No one else mentions him in relation to the restroom."

"OK. We'll put down Kichler and Wu Lin on our list and Nordlund leaving the room before and after them with a question mark." McKernan added the names to the list:

McAndrews
Fujika
Olberman
Nordlund?
Kichler
Wu Lin
Nordlund?

"Now Kichler and Gordon went to play billiards. What do the statements say about that?"

"Mr. Kichler says they left the dining room together. Gordon went ahead while Kichler went to the restroom."

"Clear enough. And the bridge players?"

Ferris looked through the statements. "Mr. DuChene says he left first to set things up. We know that Mr. Fujika went to the restroom first, so he's probably next, then Olberman, then Mr. Wu Lin." McKernan wrote down the names in that order in a list below the restroom list:

DuChene
Fujika
Olberman
Wu Lin

"I think from this we can assume that Nordlund went to the restroom after Olberman and before Kichler." The inspector erased Nordlund's name from the place before Kichler and after Olberman. "So where does that leave us?"

"We're missing the Russian, sir. Mr. Kasperovski. His statement says that he talked to the governor and then went to the library. He followed Mr. Nordlund out of the dining room."

"That clarifies things." To the other side of his floor plan McKernan wrote a new list:

Krieger – goes to Cupola
DuChene – lounge setup bridge table
McAndrews – restroom, lounge
Fujika – restroom, lounge, bridge
Olberman – restroom, lounge, bridge
Nordlund – restroom, lounge
Kasperovski – library
Tsangambo – leaves club
Gordon – billiards room
Kichler – restroom, billiards
Wu Lin – restroom, lounge, bridge

"I'm not sure about where to put the governor, but I've written him in after Kasperovski who we know was talking to him. You'll note, constable, that each of our suspects, with the exception of Gordon and Kichler, left the dining room by themselves. Those two left together but went in opposite directions. You will also note from the map, that the shortest path to any of the destinations with the exception of the front door and the library passes through the bar area. And even if you are heading to the door and library you pass within a few meters of where the port was standing."

"I can see that, sir? But what does it tell us?" Ferris asked.

"What does it tell us? It tells us everything. And nothing," McKernan added with exasperation. "From our list it would seem that each of the members at the dinner passed through or could have gone into the bar without anyone else watching them."

"What about the butler?" Ferris asked. "Where was he during this time?"

"He says that Krieger ordered his port as he left the dining room. Jeeves then went to tell Teague. Teague pours the port and then goes to the storeroom in the cellar. We know that he did this before DuChene left the dining room because DuChene noticed that Teague wasn't behind the bar. Meanwhile, Jeeves had returned to the dining room to collect glasses to return to the bar for washing. He also went around taking drink orders. When the last person had left the dining room he alerted the kitchen that the dining room was empty and they could come up to clear the tables and load the dishes into the elevator. Jeeves then took the port upstairs to the Cupola."

"So he could have gone into the bar when no one was looking?"

"Think for a moment, Ferris. It would have been a lot easier and safer for him to wait until he had gone upstairs with the port to poison it. He could have done it on the landing before opening the airlock. I think it safe to say that Jeeves is the one person who didn't poison the port while it was sitting on the bar. Of course, that doesn't mean he didn't do it just before he took it in to Krieger."

"Well, what about Alicante and the chef?"

"That's a more interesting question, constable. They were together in the kitchen. But the question is, were they together the whole time? And what about Mrs. Simpson and the custodian, Duckworth? What were they doing? No one has mentioned seeing them so far, but we know they were in the club."

"So we really haven't gotten anywhere, have we, sir?"

"I wouldn't say that. We just haven't eliminated anyone, yet. But we do have a clearer view of what order things happened in. Now, let's ask some more questions."

CHAPTER 11
MRS. SIMPSON TELLS HER STORY

"Before we get started, Ferris, did you get off those enquiries to Earth?"

"I sent a list of everyone who was in the club last night with a request for background information just like you asked sir. I marked it 'Urgent.'"

"So with luck they might get back to us in a week with half of what we asked for," the inspector commented.

"Probably," Ferris agreed dubiously. All official requests had to pass through the Trust Authority bureaucracy. The constable had been on the job long enough to understand that the needs of law enforcement on Mars were not necessarily a priority with those on Earth responsible for the planet's governance.

"Sir?"

"Yes?"

"I've got this friend back on Earth. He's pretty good at finding things in the 'cloud.' I sent him the list as well. He's unemployed right now, so he's got the time. I said we might pay him a bit if he found anything useful. Was that alright, sir?"

McKernan smiled at his constable's resourcefulness. The fact that his friend was unemployed wasn't surprising. Half the population of Earth was without a job and living on the dole. That was why there were so many people willing to come to Mars despite the conditions and dangers.

"I imagine I can squeeze a few dollars out of the budget, constable. We'll see what he turns up. Let him know that

I'll pay him if he turns up something useful. Right now we need to interview the staff. I talked to Teague the barman and Jeeves last night, but I didn't get a formal statement. Why don't you see if you can round one of them up for starters."

While Ferris was off in search of the first interviewee, McKernan reviewed the notes he had taken the night before. There really wasn't much to them except the fact that the glass of port had been left untended on the bar for some minutes, clearly enough time for someone to have slipped the cyanide into the glass. What he didn't have was a feel for the personalities involved, especially the staff. Hopefully, the interviews would clear some of that up. He was almost relieved when Ferris popped in.

"I found Teague just finishing breakfast in the staff lounge downstairs, sir," Ferris said by way of introduction.

McKernan wondered about that for a moment, but then realized that the bartender probably kept late hours on a regular basis and would be a late riser.

"Good. Have a seat, Mr. Teague. This shouldn't take long. I just have a few questions for you."

"I told you everything I know last night, Inspector," the barman said as he took the chair opposite McKernan.

"Probably. But we need to get a formal statement. Procedure, you understand. Perhaps if you could just go over the sequence of events from the time Jeeves gave you the order for the port."

Teague related essentially the same story as the one he had given the previous evening, but McKernan noted that a few of the details were different. It didn't sound as if it were a story that had been rehearsed, but more like one being told after having thought about the events further.

"Yes, that pretty much confirms what you told me last night," McKernan said. "There are a few points that aren't quite clear, though. For instance, how was it that you didn't realize that you were running low on Scotch and vodka until after the end of the dinner. Wouldn't that normally be something you would have checked on earlier?"

"You have to understand, Inspector, I don't come on duty in the bar until 1600. Normally the first thing I do is check the stock, but there were already several of the gentlemen waiting for drinks in the bar area. I served them their drinks, chatted with them a bit, you know, like bartenders do. Just small talk. At that time, there was still more than two thirds of a bottle of the Scotch."

"Do you remember which members these were?"

"Mr. Olberman and Mr. DuChene, Inspector. Well, like I was sayin' I was chatting with them and then several more came in for drinks before the dinner, it bein' Friday and all. I was kept pretty busy pourin' drinks after that until they all went in for dinner. There was a bit of a run on the Scotch which is why I needed to fetch another bottle."

"And you don't keep more than one bottle behind the bar?"

"It's kind of crowded back there, what with the glassware and coolers and such. I have to have a lot of different bottles because some like Scotch, some like Bourbon, some like rye. Then someone will have an urge for a margarita or a Cuban Libre or something odd like that so I have to have tequila and rum and the different mixers. It all takes up a lot of space. Also, a lot of the gentlemen have their own special bottles, just like Mr. Krieger had his port. That and I had all the wine for the dinner to store. There's not a lot of room left for extra bottles."

"I can see where that would be a problem," McKernan said sympathetically. "But couldn't you have run down to the storeroom during the dinner?"

"Mr. Fenton doesn't like me to leave the bar during dinner. Besides, I had to deal with the wine."

"Doesn't Jeeves take care of that?"

"Oh, he pours the wine, but I open the bottles as they are needed. Jeeves is too busy waiting on the table to deal with that."

"Well, I think that explains that. Tell me, Teague, how did you get on with Mr. Krieger?"

"Get on?" the puzzled barmen asked.

"Yes, was he an easy customer to serve?"

"Mr. Krieger didn't drink that much, Inspector. Mostly just wine with dinner and his port. He didn't spend much time in the bar, so I didn't know him as well as some of the other gentlemen. Not like Mr. Olberman, say, who is always talking about his children back on Earth."

"But when you did serve him, was he friendly?"

"No," Teague said hesitatingly. "I wouldn't say friendly like. He'd just give his order. He wasn't one for conversation. At least not with the likes of me."

"Oh?" McKernan asked sensing some uneasiness on the bartender's   part.
"I mean, staff. He was the same with Jeeves, Mrs. Simpson, even Mr. Fenton."

"So he drew class distinctions?"

"Yes, sir. Not like Mr. Olberman or Mr. Nordlund. Not that Mr. Krieger was rude or anything. Just not friendly like."

It didn't seem to McKernan that he was going to get any more along that line. "To change the topic, how did you end up on Mars?"

"Me. I was working on a cruise ship as a bartender. That was alright, but not much money. I saw an ad for this position. When I enquired, the money was fantastic and the duties light. I applied and got the job."

"Any regrets?"

"Oh, it's kind of lonely and there's not much to do, but I'm making plenty of money with nothing to spend it on. I should be able to go back home and open my own place when my contract is done."

"Well, good luck on that, Mr. Teague. I don't think I have any more questions for the moment. If I think of any, I know where I can find you."

"I guess you do," the barman said as he left.

"Well that was pretty straight forward, if not particularly enlightening," McKernan remarked after he was gone. "Why don't you see if you can round up the housekeeper next, Ferris."

The constable returned in a few minutes with Mrs. Simpson, the housekeeper. She wasn't exactly what inspector had envisioned, at least on Mars where the population tended to be in their late twenties or thirties. Mrs. Simpson was a heavyset woman who looked to be in her mid fifties with graying hair pulled back in knot at the nape of her neck. She was wearing a white apron over a gray dress with tennis shoes.

"Mrs. Simpson? I'm Chief Inspector McKernan and this is Constable Ferris."

"I know who you are, inspector," the woman answered in the accent of the north of England.

"Fine, Mrs. Simpson. You know Mr. Krieger died last night. I'd like to know where you were and what you were doing from the time the dinner ended until the body was discovered."

"Easy enough. I was in my room," she answered matter of factly.

"You weren't involved in the dinner, then?"

"No. I'm not usually, unless it's a special occasion and there's more than Mr. Watson can handle. I had my dinner at 1730 down in the staff dining room and after went to my room to watch some tele. First I heard about Mr. Krieger was when Mr. Watson came down after your lot had left."

McKernan noted with interest that Mrs. Simpson was the first person to call the Butler by his real name. "Did anyone see you during that time, or did you see anyone?"

"Well Walter, that's Walter Duckworth the janitor, had dinner at the same time as I did. Teague and Mr. Watson were already upstairs taking care of the members. But after dinner, I went to my room like I said earlier. Alone." She said the latter as if to make sure he understood there had been no improprieties.

"And Mr. Duckworth? What did he do after dinner?"

"I think he watched some tele in the lounge. There was a football game on. American style. He likes those. Personally, I can't see the attraction. All those big men bashing into each other. It's a wonder more of them don't get hurt."

The inspector had to smile at that.

"Tell me, Mrs. Simpson, if you don't mind, just how did you come to be on Mars? To satisfy my curiosity. It seems like it's a far ways from England."

"Well, it's like this, inspector. Me and my husband, Alf Simpson, rest his soul, used to run a little hotel on the coast north of York. It wasn't much, really, but it kept us going. But then Alf got himself killed in a motor accident. Run over, he was. The man never stopped, neither. They never found out who it was. Well, after that, I couldn't really run the place by meself. Not that I wanted to. So I sold it off to a young couple. They seemed nice and just startin' out so I gave them a good price. Well, I didn't know what to do next. Alf and I never had no kids or family, like. So I was looking for a position as a housekeeper at a resort hotel or something. That's about all I know to do. I just wanted to get away, I guess. Well, I saw this advert for a position as housekeeper at the Mars Club. I didn't know at the time that they actually meant on Mars like. Anyway, I applied, sent in my references and all. Well, they called about an interview, and that's when I found out they were talking about the planet Mars. It was Mr. Fenton that did the interviewing, and he offered me the job. I think he wanted someone dependable, like. At first I wasn't too keen, but then I thought to myself, 'Alice, what have you got to lose? You got no family to speak of, no ties with Alf gone. The change would do you good.' And the pay was quite good. A lot more than I could ever have expected to make back on Earth, even if I could have found a position. So I took Mr. Fenton up on the offer."

"And how is it working out for you, Mrs. Simpson?" McKernan asked.

"Not so bad. Not as exciting as I had thought, but the work isn't hard. The place isn't really all that big, not as big as our old hotel, really. And I must say the low gravity is a pleasure to my knees. Of course the dust is a problem. It seems to get into everything. You'd think they'd do something about that, wouldn't you."

McKernan could sympathize. Somehow, despite the best efforts of the engineers, the red dust from the surface managed to get past all the filters on the airlocks and coated everything with a red film that was hard to clean off.

"Did you have much to do with Mr. Krieger, Mrs. Simpson?"

"No. I hardly ever saw the man. Not that he'd have a kind word for the staff. Not like some of the gentlemen. Like Mr. McAndrews. He's always so polite. No, the only time I ever talked to Mr. Krieger was when I'd go to clean his room, and half the time he'd tell me to go away."

"You wouldn't have any idea, then, of who would want to poison Mr. Krieger?"

"Poison?" Mrs. Simpson exclaimed. "You mean he was murdered? Here, at the Mars Club? It doesn't seem possible. I know it's a bit stuffy, but it's a very respectable place."

"Well, I'm afraid someone here last night wanted him dead. They poured cyanide into his glass of port while it was sitting on the bar."

"How awful. You don't suspect me, Inspector, do you?"

McKernan shook his head with a smile. "No, I don't suspect you, Mrs. Simpson. I think that will be all the questions for now. Thank you. I'd appreciate it if you could send in Mr. Duckworth to see us."

"I'll see if I can find him. He's usually taking care of cleaning the downstairs this time of the morning," Mrs. Simpson said as she stood to leave.

After she had left Ferris asked, "You *don't* suspect her, do you?"

"I suspect everyone, constable. And they say poison is a woman's weapon," McKernan answered, but when he saw the shocked look on Ferris's face he clarified, "But, no I don't think she killed Krieger. At least not yet."

CHAPTER 12
A MAN WITH A PLAN

A firm knock on the door announced the next witness, the janitor and maintenance man, Walter Duckworth. When he entered, he was revealed to be a wiry man of middle height in his late forties or early fifties. His weathered face bore witness to a lifetime of exposure to the elements, something that obviously had occurred before he had come to Mars, where to step outside without the protection of a surface suit meant near instantaneous death.

"Have a seat, please. You're Walter Duckworth, the janitor?" McKernan began the interview.

"Janitor, maintenance man, heavy lifter and any other job no one else wants to do," Duckworth replied, apparently without any rancor. His accent was vaguely Canadian

"We've just a few questions about where you were last night."

"About the Mr. Krieger that was poisoned. Yeah, Alice told me about it." The way he said her name seemed to hint at a familiarity that had been missing during the housekeeper's interview.

"All right. Let's start with where you were?"

"Well, I had my dinner down in the staff dining room with Alice. All the other staff were working, which isn't unusual. After dinner, I watched a football game on the TV in the lounge. Green Bay at Cleveland. That ran until just after 2200. Then I went to my room, read a little bit and went to bed. I didn't hear about Krieger till I woke up in the morning. You can check on the time of the game, it was on channel B."

Evidently, Ferris had done just that. He looked up from his computer tablet and nodded at the inspector.

"And Mrs. Simpson? What did she do after dinner?"

"We both cleaned up the table. Then she went to her room to watch TV. Alice isn't terribly fond of American style football. Nor any other sports for that matter. She let me watch the game in the lounge because she knows I like to see it on the bigger screen."

"And you didn't see her after she went to her room?"

"No."

"What about anybody else? Did you see anyone while you were watching the game."

"No. Jose and Al were still working in the kitchen when I went to my room and Jeeves and Teague were working upstairs. I think I heard Teague going up after getting something from storage, but I didn't actually see him. The game was getting interesting. The Packers had just intercepted the ball and were driving for a touchdown that would put them ahead."

"When do you think you heard Teague?"

"I can't really say. I was watching the game, not the clock."

"When in the game was it?"

"Just before the end of the third quarter. I remember because they wanted to score while they had the wind at their backs. It was blowing pretty strong."

"So, say about 2130?"

"Yeah, somewhere around then. Probably a little earlier. Give or take five or ten minutes."

"And you didn't see or hear anyone else?"

"Well, occasionally I could hear some banging in the kitchen. You know, loading pots into the dishwasher, that kind of thing. You can't see into the kitchen from the lounge and I wasn't paying attention."

"Could you hear any voices from the kitchen?"

"Just Jose singing every now and then."

"But not his assistant?"

"No. But the kitchen is way at the back, so he'd have to be talking pretty loud for me to hear, especially over the game."

"Did you know Mr. Krieger at all?"

"Just by sight. I don't get upstairs that much unless a sink needs to be unclogged or something heavy needs to be moved. Alice handles most of the light cleaning upstairs. I do the cleaning down here. If there's a big party or something they'll slap a white jacket on me and give me a tray of drinks to pass around, but that's about it."

"How long have you been on Mars, Mr. Duckworth?" the inspector asked. McKernan knew the answer already, but sometimes people would let things slip when asked directly.

"Nearly six years, now. I came up as a prospector. Thought I'd make my fortune."

"And did you?" McKernan asked with a smile.

"I'm still working, aren't I. I did all right for awhile. Better than most. But I decided to quit while I was ahead. I finally had an accident that scared me silly. I punctured my suit. I'd be dead if my partner hadn't been able to slap a patch on it before all my air leaked out."

"Was that when you started working for the Mars Club?"

"No, that was a little later. My partner and I had finally had a bit of luck and we were able to sell a claim to Anglo-Martian. He cashed in his share and returned to Earth, but I decided to hang around. I prospected for a few more months, but it wasn't the same. It's too dangerous working alone and there wasn't anyone I'd trust as a new partner. I saw an ad for this job here. Well, I've been in mining and prospecting most of my life and I can fix just about anything. The pay was ok and it came with board and room. I decided to take it until something better turned up. I sold what gear I didn't need and put the money in the bank."

"You don't miss the excitement of prospecting?" McKernan queried.

"At my age excitement is over-rated," Duckworth chuckled. "The work here isn't hard and the people are ok. Alice is alright once you get to know her. Same with Al and Teague. Even Jose is ok if a little temperamental. Anyway, I'm just kind of marking time. I've got some plans that I'm working on."

That was something McKernan had heard before from some of the long timers on Mars. Things were wide open and half the people you talked to had a scheme of some sort or other to fill a niche and make a fortune. Some of them even succeeded.

"What did you do before you came to Mars."

"Worked as a miner, roustabout, rigger, whatever I could get. Mostly cold places, North Slope, northern Canada, Svalbard. Oil, coal, copper, you name it. It's not that different from Mars, really. You still got to dress up when you go outside, it's just that on Earth you can breathe the air, though at forty below you sometimes wish you didn't."

McKernan thought to himself that Dusckworth's story wasn't that different than most of the miners and prospectors on Mars. Most had worked in the Arctic or Antarctica or some other extreme environment.

"You never worked for Pretoria Mining or any company Krieger had been involved in?"

"Never worked for Pretoria. They were mostly in Africa and Antarctica before they came to Mars. As far as Krieger, not that I know of, but then a lot of those execs flip from one company to another."

"So you don't know of anyone who would have a grudge against Krieger?"

"Like I said, I really didn't know the man. But, no, I'm not aware of anyone that had it in for him."

"I'm curious, Mr. Duckworth. You mentioned that you had 'plans.' Anything you care to talk about?"

"Don't see why not. It's no big secret. I've still got a claim on a few square kilometers. It's not too far from Junction One on the road. Maybe ten kilometers from there by buggy. It's a real scenic place. The real Mars. An old wash from back when there was flowing water, a couple of small craters, that kind of thing. Just the kind of spot for tourists looking for the 'Mars' experience. I'm thinking about opening a little hotel. Nothing fancy. Put the guests up in huts, but provide them with good food and a decent bar. Rent out surface suits, offer guided buggy tours, that kind of thing. All I really need is a little more capital and the right partner, one with experience in the hotel business."

It seemed clear to Mckernan who he had in mind for a partner, though he wasn't sure Mrs. Simpson would see it the same way. It was a crazy idea, but then the sane ones had all been taken long ago. As it was, Mars already got a trickle of tourists looking for an exotic thrill. If transport between Earth and Mars got cheaper or a little faster that might develop. And half the people on Mars never got farther than Mars City and never stepped outside. Duckworth just might be on to something.

"I guess I've heard crazier ideas, Mr. Duckworth. I wish you luck."

"Thanks, inspector. I guess I'll need it. Anything else you'd like to know?"

"No, I think we've covered it. Thanks for your help. If you could send in the Jeeves, I'd appreciate it."

"Sure thing."

Jeeves knocked on the door a few moments later.

"You wished to see me, Inspector?"

"We just need to take a formal statement."

"Of course, sir. Anything I can do to be of assistance." McKernan was having a hard time deciding whether the butler was putting on an act, or if he really was as formal as he seemed. He decided it was probably a little of both. As with Teague, he had the butler retell his story or the previous nights events, and as with the barman, there was little deviation in the retelling.

Moving on, McKernan asked, "How was your relationship with Mr. Krieger?"

"Relationship, sir?"

"Was he easy to deal with? Was he demanding? Things like that."

"Mr. Krieger had very definite ideas about how he wanted things, Inspector. I tried to serve him as best I could, as I do with all the gentlemen."

"I see. Did you ever hear him have an argument with any of the other members? Or the staff?"

"I couldn't say, sir. I try not to eavesdrop on private conversations," the butler answered unhelpfully.

"So you aren't aware of anyone who might have had a grudge against Mr. Krieger?"

"Not to my knowledge, sir."

It was clear to the inspector that this line of questioning was not going to be productive.

"Have you always worked as a butler, Jeeves?"

"Oh no, sir. I worked my way up from footman to valet and then to butler, but I've been a butler for some twenty years now, sir."

"I'm curious as to how you came to work at the Mars Club. I wouldn't have thought that there was much of a demand for butlers."

"I had worked for Mr. Fenton once before. In London. When he obtained his current position he asked me if I was interested in the position of butler. As I was between employments at the time I accepted."

"Coming to Mars was a pretty drastic decision, wasn't it?"

"Unfortunately, openings for butlers are becoming quite scarce these days. The pay at the Mars Club is good and the duties are not arduous."

McKernan thought that that was becoming a theme amongst the staff of the club.

"Is there anything you can tell us that might shed some light on how the glass of port came to be poisoned?"

"I'm afraid not, Inspector. A most unfortunate incident." McKernan thought that he said that in the same tone he would have announced that the toast was burnt. There didn't seem any point in continuing.

"That will be all for now, Jeeves," McKernan said. "Could you find Chef Doro and send him in?"

"Thank you, Inspector," the butler said and left.

After he was gone, McKernan turned to Ferris and asked, "Well what do you think so far, constable?"

The younger policeman thought for a moment then replied, "It seems to me we've got two people who have no alibi and who can't provide an alibi for anyone else. Then we've got two people who we know had access to the port when no one was looking, but no obvious motive for either of them."

"That's about the size of it. Not that we've got a motive for Mrs. Simpson or Duckworth, either, but it is possible that one of them could have sneaked upstairs while Teague was in the storage room and dropped the cyanide in Krieger's port without being seen."

"That butler struck me as being kind of a cold fish," Ferris said.

"But is he a murderer?" the inspector countered.

CHAPTER 13
THE CHEF AND THE REST

Chef Duro appeared in the doorway. "Duckworth said you wish to see me?" he said a little nervously in slightly accented English. He was just under average height and somewhat on the stout side, not really fat, but it was obvious he enjoyed his own cooking. He thinning dark hair was cropped short and he was wearing a chef's jacket.

"Yes. We just have a few questions," the inspector said pleasantly. "it should only take a few minutes of your time."

"Sí. About Senor Krieger, yes?"

"Yes. Did you know the man?"

"No. Not really. Several times he had specific requests for a dish for his dinner. We spoke of that. But, no, other than professionally I did not know him."

"How long have you been chef here, Mr. Duro?"

"Nineteen months," he said with a sigh.

"You are not happy in your work?" McKernan asked.

"Do not misunderstand me. The pay is good, the duties are not severe. But for a man like me, used to fresh ingredients, seafood straight from the ocean, it is not so enjoyable. I will not be sad when I return to Earth."

"May I ask why you took this position, then?"

"The money, Inspector," he replied with a shrug. "The pay is good, and there is nothing to spend it on. I've been a cook all my life, but always in someone else's restaurant. I started out as a kitchen boy, then a prep cook, line cook, sou chef, finally chef, but always I work for somebody else.

Portugal, Spain, a cruise ship, Brazil even. Now I want to have my own restaurant. But that takes money, capital, you know. So I see the job advertisement. Three year contract with pay twice what I could hope for anywhere else. It seemed like a good idea at the time."

"And now?"

"Now I count the days till I go home. But I can't complain. I will go home with enough money in the bank to start my restaurant."

"Well, I wish you luck, chef. But we seem to have gotten off the subject. Where were you at the end of dinner last night?"

"I was in the kitchen. People think the work is done when the food is served, but no. We have to clean up, make preparations for the next day, that sort of thing."

"How late did you work?"

"Oh. I don't know. Maybe 2300."

"And you were in the kitchen all that time?"

"Yes."

"I believe that Alphonso Allicante is your assistant?"

"Yes."

"And he was in the kitchen with you?"

"Not all the time. Right after dinner he goes up to clear the tables. You see, there is a little elevator in the pantry upstairs. He puts the plates and things on a cart and sends them down. I take them from the cart in the kitchen and put them in the dishwasher machine."

"And how long did that take?"

"Not so long. There were only eight at the dinner. Maybe half an hour, a little more. Of course, he has to wait until the diners leave the dining room before he can start. Jeeves has a button he pushes to light a light in the kitchen when he is ready for us."

"Do you remember the time that your assistant went up to clear the dishes?"

"It was about 2115."

"So he rode up in the elevator with one of the carts?"

"No," Duro said with a laugh. "The elevator is small, only big enough for a cart. Alphonso took the stairs."

"And he was upstairs for a half an hour, say till 2145?"

"Yes, about then. Maybe a little later. I didn't look at a clock."

"Is there just the one cart?"

"No, we have several. Jose sends down one, I send another up. He fills it and sends it down. If he doesn't need any more carts he turns off the light. Very simple, really."

McKernan thought to himself that it did seem surprisingly low tech, yet quite effective and reliable.

"So, other than the light and the carts going up and down the elevator you and Jose aren't really in communications with each other?"

"Communications? Oh, like a radio or phone. No. Why? There is no need."

"No, I suppose not," McKernan replied. "I think I've just one more question, then. While you were alone in the kitchen, did you see anyone coming down or going up the stairs?"

"No. But then, the elevator and dishwasher are out of sight of the stairs. Wait, I did see Teague come down once. I think he was going to the storeroom for bottles."

"You don't happen to remember the time, do you?"

"No. Is it important?"

"Not really," McKernan said, though he thought otherwise. "Well, I know you are a busy man, Chef, so I will let you go now. Thank you for your help. And if you could send your assistant to us that would be helpful."

"Alphonso? Sure." The chef got up looking relieved.

The assistant chef appeared a few minutes later.

"Chef said you wished to ask me questions?" His English was not as good as the chef's. Allicante was a thin Spaniard, around thirty, dressed as his boss had been in a chef's coat and baggy white pants.

"You cleaned up after the dinner last night. Is that correct?"

"Si?"

"Do you remember what time that was?"

"After dinner," he answered as if it was a silly question.

"But what time was that?"

"I didn't notice, senor."

"How long did it take you to clean up?"

"I don't know. Until I was done."

"But how long was that?" McKernan asked with some frustration. "A half hour? Forty-five minutes? An hour?" "Not so long as an hour, senor. Maybe a half-hour, forty minutes. I have to remove the dishes, put the napkins and table cloth in a hamper for Mrs. Simpson. Wipe down the table."

"From where you were in the dining room, could you see into the bar area?"

"I'm too busy for that."

"So you didn't see anyone in the bar?"

"No. I could hear people in the hallway, but I didn't look to see. I was busy."

McKernan debated asking further questions, but decided against it. There didn't seem much point. Either the assistant's command of English was limited or he was just one of those intentionally dense individuals. In any case it didn't seem as if there was anything to be gained by extending the interview at this point.

"Thank you, Mr. Alicante. That will be all, I think."

The other looked up in surprise, then gave a shrug and left the room.

"Well, that was helpful," McKernan remarked to Constable Ferris.

"Pretty unobservant, sir," Ferris replied.

"To be fair, he was working and not expecting a murder to be taking place just outside the room."

"He could have slipped out to the bar and dropped the cyanide into the glass," Ferris said. "No one would notice. They would just think he was doing his work."

"Do you think he did it?" McKernan asked.

"No," Ferris replied with a smile.

"So where does that leave us?" the inspector asked as much to the air as to the constable.

Fenton, the club steward, chose that moment to pop his head into the room. "I was just wondering if you would like me to send in some lunch, inspector? I'm afraid we don't usually put on much of a feed at lunch on Saturday. Just soup and sandwiches."

"That would be fine, Fenton," McKernan answered, suspecting that the steward had made the offer to keep them out of the dining room and the view of the members. "But while you are here, perhaps you could answer a few questions."

"Of course, inspector. What do you wish to know?"

"Where were you from the end of the dinner until Jeeves informed you about Mr. Krieger?"

"Well, it's my habit at the end of dinner after coffee has been served to step into the dining room to make sure everything was satisfactory."

"So you weren't at the dinner, yourself?"

"No," Fenton answered as if the inspector had made a most improper suggestion. "I usually have a tray in my office."

So he doesn't eat with the help, either, McKernan noted.

"I had a few words with the governor as things were breaking up. He thanked me for the meal and asked me to give my compliments to the chef. That sort of thing. I stood around making small talk until the dining room cleared out, and then went to my office. That's right behind the front vestibule."

"Do you remember what time that was?"

"2120, I believe."

"Did you see the governor leave?"

"Yes. Or almost, at least. I saw him heading down the corridor next to the dining room towards the front door." It struck McKernan not for the first time, how everyone in the club insisted on referring to it as a "door" rather than the airlock "hatch" that it was.

"But you didn't actually see him go through the door?"

"No. I walked through the bar. You see, the door to my office is behind the desk in the vestibule. I walked down the corridor on the other side, the one that runs past the lounge."

"Did you notice if the glass of port was sitting on the bar when you went through?"

"It was not. Nor was Teague behind the bar. I assumed he was getting something from the stockroom. He's a good bartender, but he lacks organization at times."

"After you were in your office, did you happen to note anyone stepping into the bar?"

"I'm afraid not. I had my door shut. I was working on the accounts for the month and I wanted some peace and privacy. I didn't see anyone else until Jeeves came and knocked on my door."

"Did you note the time?"

"I'm afraid not. I do know that it was 2207 when I informed Mr. McAndrews, so it was only a minute or two before that."

"Thank you. That's helpful," McKernan said as he noted the time. "I think that will be all for the moment."

"If you like, I'll have lunch sent in," Fenton said as he stood to leave.

"That would be appreciated," McKernan replied, anticipating the quality of the food at the Mars Club.

After the secretary left McKernan asked of Ferris, "Does it strike you as curious, constable, that every single member of the staff was all alone at the time the port was poisoned? Alicante could have done it when he came up to clear. Or, once he came up, he could have slipped out of the dining room at any time until the butler took the port up. Similarly, the chef *could* have waited until Alicante was up clearing and then come up the stairs. There would have been a short window where either of them could have done it, short, but probably long enough. The other two on the lower level, Mrs. Simpson and Duckworth could have done it any time while Teague was in the storeroom."

"Or maybe they all just had work to do at that time. Or were off duty," Ferris replied.

"Yes, it could be that—" McKernan's retort was interrupted by a knock on the door as Jeeves brought in the lunch tray. The sandwiches were pastrami and Swiss cheese on caraway rye. The soup was cream of broccoli. Jeeves had thoughtfully included two glasses of beer. Upon tasting, McKernan decided the beer had probably been brewed in Munich. One of the oddities of life on Mars was that with transportation costs, it rarely was worth importing anything but the best.

CHAPTER 14
RECONSTRUCTIONS

After a very satisfying lunch McKernan sat back and asked his underling, "Well, constable, what do you think?"

"Sir?"

"We've reviewed the statements from all the members as to their motions last night and this morning we've interviewed the staff that were in the lower level. What conclusions have you drawn from that, Ferris?"

"Well, for one thing, I'm not sure all the times agree," Ferris replied.

"You've noticed that. It's not surprising, in a way. No one was expecting that they'd have to be precise. People are often very bad at gauging time. I think we have to take all of the times as approximate. What we really have to concern ourselves with is the relative timing of events, how things happen in relation to each other, particularly as it relates to Teague's trip to the cellar."

"That makes sense, sir."

"We can assume that Teague the barman and Jeeves the butler would have had no difficulty in putting the potassium cyanide into the port without being observed. Can we say the same of anyone else? Conversely, is there anyone that we can rule out?"

"I see what you're getting at, sir. Well, we have all the gentleman who used the restroom after dinner. They all seem to have gone while Teague was away. They would have passed through the bar area as the shortest path—"

"And as we both know that after a lengthy dinner with several drinks that would have been a prime concern," the inspector remarked wryly.

A bit flustered by the interruption, constable Ferris continued. "Yes. They would have passed through the bar and, presuming that they had the poison on them it shouldn't have take more than a few seconds to add it to the port as it sat on the bar."

"I think we can take it for granted that this was a premeditated crime, Ferris. It may not have been planned out in detail, but the murderer came to dinner with the idea of killing Krieger. He knew his habits, knew that Krieger was likely to order a port to be delivered to the Cupola, and so came prepared with the potassium cyanide."

"But how could he know that Teague would be away from the bar leaving the port on the table?" Ferris objected.

"Oh, I don't think our killer did. That was just a fortuitous event from the his standpoint. Of course, for us it causes problems because we have a period of several minutes when various parties are traipsing through the bar seemingly in single file so that they were all out of sight of anyone while passing the port. I suspect that the original plan was to stand at the bar as if ordering a drink and wait until Teague was distracted, or barring that divert his attention by asking him something that required him to turn to the back bar. The fact that Teague went down to the stockroom in the cellar just made things easier."

"So you think the murderer was one of the men that went to the restroom?"

"I don't think we can confine our suspicions to them. Look at the layout of this place. Everyone was in the dining room. Afterwards, they all end up in either the lounge, the billiards room, or in the case of Mr. Kasperovski, the library. The most convenient route to either the lounge or the billiards room is through the bar. The alternatives are either the rear hallway or through the front vestibule, both of which are far less direct. Even our Russian would have passed right by the bar on his way to the library. Going in would have only added a few steps. The problem for us is that they all seem to have made their ways singly rather than in groups, so none of the members has an alibi for the entire period."

"And the same line of reasoning that applies to Kasperovski applies to Mr. Fenton, wouldn't it, sir?"

"Unfortunately, you're right about that, Ferris. And presumably the governor as well, though we haven't had a chance to interview him yet."

"Do you think we can rule out the staff who were on the lower level?"

"Can we? They were each isolated in a different room at the time with videos playing or machinery going. How long do you think it would take to come up the stairs go into the bar area and return?"

"I don't know, sir? A few minutes, I'd guess."

"Probably less. And the head of the stairs is just around the corner from the bar."

"So what do we do, sir? You seem to be saying that anyone who was in the club last night could have done it. Even the governor!"

"Don't worry, constable. I'm not ready to accuse his Excellency just yet. But what we have so far are just suppositions. Maybe we should put them to the test."

"I don't think I follow you, sir," Ferris said puzzled.

"I think we should time just how long it does take to execute each of the hypothetical paths our murderer might have taken including the few seconds it would take to spike the port."

"Sir?"

"We're going to attempt to recreate the crime, Ferris. They do it in all the best detective stories, you know."

"If you say so, sir," Ferris said dubiously.

"I do. Come on, constable. Let's start with the time from the dining room to the restroom."

Once in the bar area, McKernan positioned himself at the end of the bar.

"Alright. Stand just inside the dining room doorway. When I give the word walk through the bar at a normal pace, pretend to reach into your jacket for an envelope with the cyanide, tip it into a glass—" the inspector reached over the bar and grabbed a tumbler which he placed on the bar, "—and then walk to the restroom door. I'll time you using my comm unit."

Ferris positioned himself as directed.

"Go!"

Ferris approached the bar, reached into his mythical jacket for the hypothetical poison, tapped his finger twice on the rim of the glass, and then continued on to the restroom.

"Not bad. Twenty-five seconds. Now let's try it in the opposite direction. Go."

"Twenty-three seconds. You're getting better at this, constable," McKernan quipped. Subsequent trials from the dining room to the lounge and from the dining room to the billiards room yielded times of twenty-one and twenty-eight second respectively. It would have taken Fenton no more than thirty seconds to reach the door of his office off the vestibule and about the same length of time for Kasperovski to walk to the library.

"Well that certainly would seem to be feasible. We had six members use the restroom, DuChene going straight to the lounge to get ready for bridge, and the two playing billiards. None of them would have needed a window of opportunity of more than half-a-minute to poison the port."

"What I don't understand is why they all seem to have crossed through the bar one at a time? It's almost as if they had it planned, sir."

"It could just be a coincidence, Ferris. An inconvenient one for us, but still, just a coincidence. And remember, these are gentlemen. They don't queue up in the hall waiting to use the toilet. They were probably watching each other out of the corner of their eye gauging when the restroom would be free. I checked earlier, and it only has the one urinal."

"What next, sir?" Ferris asked.

"I think we need to do the same thing for the people in the lower level. Why don't you go to the foot of the stairs. When I give the word come up the stairs as quietly as you can. At the top, check to see that the bar is empty, walk to the bar, poison the drink and go back down the stairs."

Several repeats of this exercise gave times of around forty seconds. Starting from the staff quarters added only another five seconds.

After the last trial, Ferris, a bit winded, asked, "So, where does this leave us, sir?"

"About where I was afraid it would. Based on our little reconstructions I don't think we can rule out anyone as a suspect."

"Even Mrs. Simpson? I don't see how she could get up those stairs as fast as I could."

"I think you'd be surprised, Ferris. I doubt if it would take her more than fifty seconds to do the deed."

"So where does that leave us?"

"Pretty much where we started, I think. What would you do next, constable?"

"We've heard from a number of people that there is plenty of potassium cyanide available on Mars, sir, but we haven't actually found out if any of it has gone missing. I think we should check with all the laboratories and see if any of them have some that's unaccounted for."

McKernan smiled to himself. Ferris was showing signs of a growing self-confidence. "That's sounds like an excellent idea, constable. I'll put you in charge of that part of the investigation. For my part, I'm going to try to obtain an interview with our governor. But before you run off to track down the cyanide I think we should check out Krieger's room, not that I expect to find anything."

CHAPTER 15
IN THE DEAD MAN'S CHAMBERS

The previous evening McKernan had asked Fenton to make sure the room was locked and remained undisturbed by anyone including the housekeeper. He had then taken custody of the key.

The upper floor of the Mars Club contained a number of small apartments used by visiting members and by those members who's corporations did not provide executive housing. Fenton had informed him that the second floor had a total of eight suites and several smaller rooms used for temporary guests. In addition to Krieger, Olberman, Fujika, Kichler, Kaperovski, and Gordon were currently residing at the club. The other members had apartments provided by their various companies or had made other arrangements for living quarters.

Krieger had been living more or less permanently in Number 3. A small, neatly letter placard in a holder on the door proclaimed it as the rooms of Mr. Peter Krieger.

McKernan inserted the key and opened the door a after turning on the light and giving it a quick examination entered. Ferris followed on his heels. By Earth standards, the apartment would have been nothing much, about what one would expect from a mid-level hotel catering to business travelers. There was a small sitting room with several comfortable chairs and a small desk. Beyond this was a bedroom with a double bed, a dresser and a nightstand. At the rear was a small bathroom equipped with a shower and a closet. There was an entertainment screen on the walls of both the sitting area and the bedroom. It was hardly what one would expect for a top executive, except that this was Mars where living space was at a premium and nearly everything had to be brought from Earth at great expense. On Mars, two rooms *en suite* was the pinnacle of luxury.

When McKernan had first come to Mars, the Trust Authority had housed him in a three by four meter cubicle with shared bath facilities with nothing for furnishings except a bed, a set of shelves and a wall mounted rod for hanging clothes. And he had been fairly senior in the ranking of Trust Authority personnel at the time. The lack of privacy and Spartan accommodations had been the primary reason that he had moved out to Hut Town when the opportunity had presented itself.

"Why don't you take the closet and the bathroom while I check the rest," McKernan said.

He hadn't expected to find much, but it looked as if they might be disappointed even in that. Krieger, it appear, was beyond neat. The sitting room was without personal touches other than a bottle of Scotch and two glasses sitting on the desk. The desk itself had three drawers, one shallow one in the middle and two deeper ones to one side. The shallow drawer contained two pens, three pencils, a ruler and a pad of paper. The top drawer on the side had another pad of paper, a calculator and a case with a pair of reading glasses. The bottom drawer was empty. Neither pad of paper had anything written on it. The waste basket next to the desk was empty. The only thing on the table between the two chairs was a lamp.

When he checked the nightstand next to the bed he found a mystery novel and an Afrikaaner bible. For the sake of thoroughness he riffled through the pages of both but no papers fell out. A search of the dresser revealed socks, underwear, a stack of shirts and not much else. He could see into the closet which Ferris was examining, but all he saw were some pants and a pair of suit jackets hanging from the rod and several pairs of shoes on the floor.

There was no sign of a surface suit or the long underwear one usually wore under it. McKernan found it hard to believe that a man with Krieger's hands on background wouldn't own one, but it was quite likely that it was stored at Pretoria Mining's office.

"Find anything in the bathroom?"

"Toothpaste, soap, shaving gear, a hair brush and comb. There were several towels and washcloths, too."

"No note admitting his sins and saying he 'was going to end it all,' I take it?"

"No, sir. I did find this in the closet, though," Ferris said, with a note of faint triumph.

This proved to be a photo album, McKernan discovered as he opened the book the constable handed him. He paged through it with Ferris peering over his shoulder.

There were about fifty pages in the album, most of which were covered in photos of various sizes. The pictures, judging from the backgrounds, were from a variety of places on Earth, most of which seemed to be mining operations in Africa and South America. There were very few people in the pictures, though occasionally there would be a group photo, usually posed in front of some large piece of mining equipment. Dates and locations had been neatly written in below each photo. None was older than about fifteen years. If McKernan had been hoping to gain some insight from Krieger's childhood or school days, he was to be disappointed.

"Not much here, is there, sir?" Ferris said as the inspector closed the album.

"No, there isn't. I'm afraid Mr. Krieger's past must remain a mystery for the moment. I don't see much point in checking for fingerprints. There's no sign that anyone other than Krieger and the housekeeper have been in here recently. You might as well start your search for missing poisons. I'll hang around here for a bit and see if I can catch any of the members who were at the dinner."

After Ferris had left, McKernan gave the room one last inspection to see if there was anything they had missed. This drew a blank. Martian construction practices, even those of the Mars Club, didn't lend themselves to secret hiding places. McKernan was about to call it quits when he received not one, but two calls on his communicator.

The first was from the governor's office granting the inspector an interview with the governor later that afternoon. McKernan was surprised that that his request had been answered at all, let alone as promptly as it had.

The second call was from Dr. Greenwood.

"I've finished my autopsy of your victim, McKernan, or at least what passes for one on Mars. I'll be filing an official report, of course, but I thought I'd let you know what I've found."

"I appreciate that, doctor," McKernan. As a doctor, Greenwood was the best Mars had to offer, but he also could be difficult to work with at times, with a tendency to be unconcerned with anyone's priorities except his own.

"As I told you earlier, there is no question that the cause of death was acute cyanide poisoning with the poison being administered orally. As the sample of port I analyzed was liberally laced with the stuff, I think you have no need to look further than that for the source of the poison. The contents of his stomach hadn't really had a chance to digest, and none of the samples I analyzed showed any sign of cyanide except what you'd expect it to have absorbed in the stomach."

"Thank you, doctor. I don't think either one of us is surprised by your findings, but it is helpful to me to rule out other possible sources. Not that it makes my job much easier."

"They may not have any bearing on the case, but I did find a few curious things in the post-mortem."

McKernan recognized this as Greenwood's attempt at humor. "Curious in what way, doctor."

"Well, one is that Mr. Krieger had suffered a gunshot wound sometime in the past. I'd say twenty or more years ago. It was a superficial to the upper left arm. From the looks of it I'd say a high-velocity round rather than from a pistol or revolver."

"In other words a military style weapon," McKernan responded. "Any chance it was from a hunting rifle? Krieger was from South Africa."

"I'm no expert on such matters, inspector, but if I had to guess I'd say something like an assault rifle rather than a sporting gun."

"Interesting," McKernan remarked. "You said you had found several curious features."

"Yes. Your Mr. Krieger had undergone plastic-surgery to his face sometime in the past. Again, twenty some years ago if I had to make an estimate."

"Are you saying that Krieger had suffered an accident in the past?" the inspector asked, suddenly curious to learn more about the victim's past.

"I'd say the nature of the surgery was more cosmetic rather than reconstructive. There's no indication of trauma to the underlying bone structure. It looks like Mr. Krieger had a nose job and some minor alterations done on his cheek bones."

"Twenty years ago Krieger would have been in his thirties. A little young for a face lift, don't you think, doctor?"

"You never know, inspector. I'll leave the inferences to you, but my medical opinion is that twenty odd years ago, Mr. Krieger tried to change his appearance."

"Anything else, doctor?"

"Only that the victim was quite fit for a man his age and probably had led a very active life."

"Well, thank you again, doctor. You've certainly given me food for thought."

McKernan sat there after the doctor had disconnected wondering just exactly who Mr. Krieger had been.

CHAPTER 16
THE DOSSIERS IN THE CASE

A quick check with Fenton revealed that none of the members who had been present the night of the dinner were currently in the Mars Club. Presumably they were all at work. Even the biggest of corporations couldn't afford to send someone to Mars just to be a figurehead. Instead, a posting to Mars was often a stepping stone to top management, that is if the candidate didn't mess up badly.

McKernan would have to postpone his interviews until later. What he could do was review what information was on file. He retired to the room where he had conducted the morning interviews, shut the door and turned on his computer tablet.

Kenji Fujika had given him a rough idea of what each of the members had been doing after dinner. Kenji, he felt he knew well enough that he didn't need to review his file. The other three that he had been playing bridge with were Stan Olberman, Wu Lin, and Frances DuChene. He might as well start with them.

He brought up the file of each and read through them. Unfortunately, there wasn't much information in the records. It was surprising, in a way. Most of the people who came to Mars, whether as employees of the Trust Authority or one of the corporations had relatively detailed files including employment histories, educational transcripts, medical and psychological evaluations and any criminal records. Evidently, the corporations, where their top executives were involved, considered this level of detail privileged information. The basics were there, date and place of birth, degrees received, the results of their pre-Mars physical, and the positions each had held within their respective corporations, but almost nothing in the way of details. What he was able to glean from the files could be distilled as follows:

Stan Olberman – An American, age 42, born in Minnesota. He was the local manager for Transamerican Minerals, a company that he had worked for since being recruited after having received a masters degree in geology. Evidently, the company had recognized his talents early on in his career and he had gone on to earn an M.B.A. while working for Transamerican. He had held a variety of positions with that company, each one with more responsibility than the last. It looked as if he was about to make the final step to top management upon his return to Earth. He had been on Mars nearly three years, which was quite a long time for someone in his position. He was married with two daughters, ages 15 and 17.

From what McKernan knew, Transamerican was one of the smaller mining companies on Mars, a bit of a late-comer to the planet. The claims that they were working were in general not as high grade as those of other companies, though they had been aggressively trying to improve on that.

Francois DuChene – age 38, born in Lyon, France. Married, one child. An engineer, he had earned several degrees in space engineering from the Ecole Polytechnique. He was the head of operations for European Space Ventures, a post he had occupied for eighteen months. Before that, he had worked on the moon and one of the new asteroid projects.

E.U.V. wasn't a mining company, but instead performed various contract services for the Trust Authority and corporations. This had included building much of the more permanent parts of Mars City and the road which extended for several thousand kilometers in either direction from the city. Their employees were a pretty cosmopolitan bunch recruited not only from Europe, but also Asia and the Americas. McKernan knew them as a serious, hard-working bunch whose worst failings were getting a bit boisterous whenever they gathered to view the rebroadcast of an important soccer match.

Wu Lin "Charlie" – age 45, married, one son. Born in Beijing. He had a degree in geology from a lesser Chinese university and then had gone on to earn a master's degree in mining engineering from the University of Sydney, in Australia. He was married with a son, age 9. His position was head of Martian operations for the People's Celestial Minerals Corporation.

Celestial Minerals had been on Mars almost from the beginning as well as having operations on the moon and several of the asteroids. They had gotten their start in Africa, but had withdrawn from there during a period of political unrest. Local resentment of Chinese "exploitation" had caused the toppling of more than one African leader that had been seen as too close to the Chinese. Presumably, they found Mars, with no indigenous population, more congenial. Celestial Minerals kept only a token office at Mars City, with most of their employees based at one of their mining compounds. The miners rarely came to the city for relaxation, instead, going to a recreation complex maintained by the company at one of the mining camps. There were rumors that Celestial was operated as a subsidiary of the Chinese People's Army, but officially there were no ties between the two.

While those three had been playing bridge, two of the members, Robert Gordon and Leo Kichler, had adjourned to the billiard room for a game. McKernan had never played pool or billiards much back on Earth, but he wondered how the lower gravity on Mars affected the game. Did they compensate by weighting the balls?

Robert Gordon – 41, born in Edmonton, Canada. Married, two children, both girls, ages 11 and 13. Mining and business degrees from Michigan Tech. He was employed by Northern and Big Sky Mining where he had worked his way up through the corporate ranks at mines in Alberta, Montana, and Baffin Island. He had been on Mars for two years.

From what the inspector had seen, Big Sky played by the rules, earned a steady profit for its share-holders and tried not to make waves. He'd met Gordon on a number of occasions and found the man friendly and pleasant.

Leo Kichler – 47, born in Buenos Aires. Married, no children. His wife was Irish. The usual degrees in mining and administration. He was the local head of Rio Plata Mining. He had only been on Mars for six months.

McKernan had only met the man once, and he hadn't made much of an impression, average height and looks, hadn't talked much. From a previous case the inspector knew that Rio Plata was a closely held family owned corporation. They were relative new-comers to Mars, but seemed to be making their investment pay.

That left the three remaining members, Boris Kasperovski, Helmut Nordlund, and Otis McAndrews. The inspector didn't have to consult the file on McAndrews. The head of Anglo-Martian had been an old Mars hand even when McKernan had first come to Mars. He knew that he had been born in Aberdeen and educated at the Imperial College in London. He also considered him someone he could trust. As to the others:

Helmut Nordlund – 43, married. He was unusual in that his wife was with him on Mars. They had a son, 16, who was back on Earth at school. He had been born in Denmark where he had studied business and administration. He had gone on to work for several airlines before taking a position with Interplanetary Transport, the company responsible for operating the spaceships that provided the lifeline between Mars and Earth.

Nordlund was a competent, affable man who enjoyed eating and drinking in moderation. As head of Interplanetary's operations on Mars he was the man responsible for scheduling and maintaining their ships, handling passengers and cargo, and for all practical purposes managing the spaceport, though technically, that was a Trust Authority facility.

Boris Kasperovski – 41, born in Moscow. Unmarried. No children. He had degrees in engineering and mining from the University of Moscow. He had been on Mars for nearly a year as the head of the Siberian Mining Conglomerate.

The one time that McKernan had met him at a reception, he had found the Russian's English to be fairly minimal. Siberian Mining was a quasi-governmental entity, one of those curious relics of the Russian tendency to periodically embrace and then reject capitalism. Like the Chinese, they largely operated in isolation, though because of their smaller size they were forced to rely on private contractors more often.

After finishing his examination of the records, McKernan found himself little better off than before. There was nothing in the files that pointed towards any of the members as a suspect. At least officially, there was nothing indicating that any of them had ever had more than incidental contact with Krieger, nor was there anything to indicate that any of them were capable of murder.

Frustated, he turned to the file on Krieger, though he had briefly looked at it before. Reading over it again, he found little of relevance. His age was given as 52. He had been born in Johannesburg. From then until approximately fifteen years ago there were no entries, nothing about education or employment. At that time he had joined Pretoria Mining, apparently as one of the founders and major share-holders. Despite the name, they seemed to have operated mostly in South America until moving off-planet to Mars five years earlier. Unlike most of the other members of the Mars Club, Krieger had already ascended to the board room. Over the last few years he had made a practice of taking up residence on the Mars for periods of four to six months at a time to oversee local operations before returning to Earth. Given the expense and the considerable time lost in transit, this was a highly unusual arrangement. Still, there was nothing in the file to provide either a motive or a suspect for his murder.

There remained one more file to examine, that of Fenton, the club steward. While he didn't think him a likely candidate for a murderer, McKernan decided he had to at least go through the motions. It turned out that Howard Fenton, 45, had been born in London. He had not attended any of the better schools, but had earned a degree in hotel administration from one of the more provincial universities. He had taken a job as night manager with a prominent hotel chain, worked his way up to manager before taking a position as steward with a private London club. This was followed in succession by several other similar positions. There was nothing in the record to indicate his reasons for changing jobs so frequently. Had he left for more money? Or had there been some sort of conflict with staff or membership? The record was unclear. Then, right before he had taken the position with the Mars Club, there had been a period of nine months when he had seemingly been unengaged. The inspector found that curious. It seemed unlikely that a man in Fenton's position would have had the means or savings to take an extended vacation, particularly during what must have been his years of prime earning potential. Was there something worth investigating there?

McKernan was considering the question when he noted the time. He had an appointment, one for which it would not do to be late.

CHAPTER 17
THE GOVERNOR GRANTS AN AUDIENCE

Though McKernan had been in the offices of several of the predecessors of the current Trust Authority Governor, he had not had that pleasure with the holder of that position. When he showed up for his appointment at the Trust Authority's building he found that Tsangambo had taken advantage of the recent enlargement of that facility to occupy a new and larger suite.

On giving his name, the receptionist asked him to take a seat and told him that she would inform the governor of his presence. The receptionist was a black woman, from one of the East African countries by her accent, presumably brought to Mars by the governor in return for a substantial boost in pay grade and the promise of a much better position upon her return to Earth. Given the typically short terms served by the governors, McKernan thought it doubtful that she had signed the normal three year contract.

McKernan had no sooner settled himself in one of the admittedly very comfortable chairs in the waiting area when a buzzer sounded on the receptionist's desk and she indicated that he could go on through to the governor's office. This room, while not quite as opulent as the Mars Club, was anything but plain and was far larger than needed. While Mars was considered a hardship post, the inspector thought that the governor was not taking that aspect too personally. The governor himself, sat behind an impressive mahogany desk in a very expensive Danish desk chair covered in what looked like real leather. A sofa and large entertainment unit were positioned to one side. Various artifacts which McKernan took to be African were arrayed around the walls. Behind the governor's desk was the flag, not of the U.N. or the Trust Authority, or even the governor's native country, but of the pan-African Revolutionary Party.

"Ah, Chief Inspector McKernan," the governor said, not bothering to stand. "Please, take a seat." He motioned towards one of the chrome and leather chairs arrayed in front of his desk. McKernan noted as he sat that the legs were just a fraction too short for comfort and put the occupant at a level lower than the governor who was already quite a tall man.

"Thank you for seeing me, Governor," McKernan said.

"I take it that this is in reference to the Krieger incident?" The governor's accent, while it still carried a hint of his native land spoke more of Oxford than the veldt.

"Yes, sir. I have a few questions to ask you."

"You believe, then, that he died not by his own hand as they say?"

"No, sir. I do not believe that Mr. Krieger committed suicide, though I haven't completely ruled that out. If he did poison his port, he did it in a particularly neat manner leaving no trace behind. There were no signs of poison found on his person or in the Cupola room."

"And so, deciding that it is a case of murder, you come to question the only black man in sight. What more natural when a prominent Afrikaaner is killed than to suspect the African nationalist. I am honored to be your prime suspect, inspector."

McKernan was having a hard time deciding whether the governor was baiting him, was just having a jest, or was deadly serious.

"At the moment I have no prime suspect, Governor. Other than the fact that a certain number of people were present at the dinner last evening, I have no suspects at all. What I am trying to do as a matter of police routine, is interview each of the people present to establish their actions in the period between the time the dinner ended and the body was discovered, and to find out what they can tell me of the movements of the other parties involved."

"So, inspector, this is just matter of police routine?"

As the governor seemed determined to play the part of a hostile witness, McKernan decided to play along.

"Exactly, Governor. Perhaps, we could start with you going over your own movements from the point the dinner ended until you left the Mars Club."

"I was seated, as you probably are aware, at the head of the table as the guest of 'honor.' At the end of the meal after the coffee, I stood up. Most of the other members took that as a cue to do the same. A few sycophants came up to me to say how much they appreciated my presence at the table or some such. Frankly, I go only because the food is so good. The chef is very talented and it allows me to stretch the meager allowance the Trust Authority provides me. But getting back to your question, I talked to a few of the members in the dining room, I can't remember which. I said my good-byes and left. On the way out I stopped to thank Fenton and his staff for the dinner. Then I left."

"Approximately how long was it after the end of dinner before you left the club?"

"Oh, I don't know," the governor replied impatiently. "Five, no, probably more like ten minutes."

"And during that time you didn't adjourn to the rest room or pass through the bar?"

"No, certainly not. I left the club as soon as I decently could. Why do you ask?"

"It seems likely, sir, that the poison was introduced into the glass of port while it sat on the bar waiting for the butler to take it up to the Cupola. As you know, the most convenient route from the dining room to the restroom is through the bar."

"Well, you can rest assured that I did not avail myself of the facilities. Of that I am certain."

"Did you notice if anyone else did?"

"I do not pay attention to who heeds the call of nature, inspector. It is a matter of complete indifference to me."

"In this case, I wish I could say the same for myself, governor. One more question, sir. When you left the club, did you take the corridor that runs along the dining room to the door, or did you use the one that runs past the lounge?"

"I don't know. The corridor by the dining room I would imagine. I exited the room and turned left. Does that satisfy you, inspector? I did not go through the bar and I did not pass the poisoned port."

McKernan sensed that the questions and answers were now becoming a game with the governor. A game he saw no point in continuing. "Unless you can think of anything else that might have a bearing on the case, governor, I think you've answered all my questions. Thank you for your time." He started to rise.

The governor seemed taken off base by the sudden termination of the interview, probably because it had not ended on his terms. "You haven't asked me how well I knew the deceased, inspector. Or if I had any motive for murder?"

"Very well, governor. How well did you know Peter Krieger? And did you have a motive for his murder?"

The governor gave a dry chuckle at his bluff being called.

"The fact is, I didn't know the man at all. In fact, the two of us had never spoken. Nor did I have any motive for wishing him dead, except for the history of his ancestors and their role in pillaging the continent of Africa."

"Then I think we are done, sir. Again, thank you for your time."

"Wait, inspector," the governor said holding up a hand with extraordinarily long fingers. "I said I didn't know Krieger. I didn't say that I didn't know *of* him."

"Is there something you think I should know, sir?" McKernan asked.

"That is for you to judge, inspector. Do you have time for a little history lesson?"

"I am at your disposal, governor."

"Very well. Sit yourself back down, inspector."

McKernan resumed his seat.

"Tell me, inspector, did you ever hear of 17 Commando?"

"I can't say that I have, sir."

"How much, then, do you know about the 'New Rhodesian War?'"

"Not much. I was pretty young at the time, still in school. It was one of the conflicts in Southern Africa, wasn't it? There were a lot of them in that era, as I remember."

"Yes, there were. Mostly about fighting corruption and combating attempts to exploit the people. I was a young man, at that time, too, but farther north, and I took part in the struggle to free my people. But the Rhodesian War was something different. It was an attempt to reestablish a white dominated state in part of the richest section of Africa. Most of the participants were descendants of

Afrikaaners, the old Boers if you will, or paid mercenaries along with some disaffected traitors who were fighting along tribal lines. It was a particularly nasty war, and there were atrocities committed on both sides, but the worst offenders were a group that called themselves 17 Commando for reasons known only to themselves."

"And this is relevant why, sir?" McKernan asked.

"Because I believe that Peter Krieger was the leader of 17 Commando."

"And you know this how, sir?"

"As I said, I didn't take part in the Rhodesian War. I was farther north, but I have friends who were there. It was from one of them that I learned this bit of information. Not that I have any proof, of course. If I did, Krieger would have been prosecuted for crimes against humanity. But as I have said, I have no proof. Just suspicions."

"And you think someone from Krieger's past might have wanted to kill him?"

"17 Commando was pretty indiscriminant during the war. There were many killed, and not just on the other side. Many innocent people were injured during the conflict. But when the war ended, 17 Commando disappeared, or at least the leaders. And they were very good at covering their tracks. But they managed to take quite a bit of loot with them, mostly in the form of diamonds. With the proceeds from their sale they could afford to buy new identities and set themselves up in business."

"I see. Do you know of anyone here on Mars who might have been involved in this Rhodesian War? Who might have a grievance?"

"Again, it was a long time ago, inspector, over twenty years, and people don't go around advertising that they were involved. But you might ask your good friend Otis McAndrews what he knows about it."

"Otis?" McKernan asked in surprise.

The governor seemed to have realized that he might have said too much. McAndrews was a powerful man with many friends. "It is not for me to say, inspector. But ask him."

"I will, governor. Is there anyone else I should know about?"

"Not that I know about, but then I don't keep track of such matters. That's your job, isn't it. That's what the Trust Authority pays you for."

"Yes it is," McKernan said. Rising again he said, "Thank you again for your time, Governor. And your candor."

This time the governor rose from his chair. "I trust I am no longer your 'prime suspect' then, inspector."

"No," the inspector said as he left the room, "not my *prime* suspect." He let the door close behind him, smiled at the receptionist and left the building.

CHAPTER 18
STAN THE MAN

His interview with the governor had left McKernan with a lot to think about, not the least of which was the implication that Otis McAndrews might be concealing something that had a bearing on the case. When they had discussed the case, Otis had denied having known Krieger in Africa. Or had he? Thinking back, he had answered the inspectors question with something about "Africa being a big place" and his time there "long ago." Not exactly a direct answer. At the time McKernan had thought that McAndrews was merely being reserved, but there might had been a hint of something more.

Whatever Otis had meant or what he was concealing by his comment, McKernan was beginning to think that the solution to the mystery lay in Krieger's past. Tsangambo certainly seemed to think so, and if his revelation that Krieger had been part of this 17 Commando were true, then that might provide ample motive for someone to have killed the man. He, himself, had been barely a teenager when the so called Rhodesian War had been going on, but from what he could remember it had been a particularly nasty conflict while it lasted. It had started as an attempt by a small group of mercenaries to turn back the clock to a time when the white man had ruled Africa. Taking advantage of the chaos that was post-Mugabe Zimbabwe and leveraging rivalries between various ethnic groups, the rebel forces had created a two year reign of terror before finally being put down by African Union troops. A lot of people had died in those two years, most of them non-combatants, enough to leave plenty of grudges.

But what was McAndrews' connection to the conflict? He'd have to create an opportunity to question McAndrews more closely about his experiences in Africa.

It was nearly 1700 when McKernan left the Trust Authority offices. With the hope of catching some of the members to continue his interviews, he returned to the Mars Club. In at least one case, it would appear he was in luck, for as he was passing the bar he saw that Stan Olberman was leaning on the bar, a drink in front of him.

"Well, if it isn't our local sleuth, chief inspector McKernan. Can I buy you a drink, inspector?"

From the slight slur in his speech, McKernan suspected that it might not be Olberman's first drink of the day. It also might prove to be a good time to ask a few questions.

"Thank you, sir. I'd appreciate that," McKernan said, moving to the bar next to Olberman.

Draining his own glass, Olberman said, "Teague, my good man, a bourbon on the rocks for the inspector. And another one for me while you're at it. On my tab."

"Yes, sir. Coming right up," the barman said. He put some ice in two glasses and poured the whiskey into the glasses. McKernan noticed that he was more generous with inspector's glass than Olberman's. Setting the drinks in front of them, Teague said, "If you gentlemen don't need anything else at the moment, I need to fetch something from the cellar."

After he had gone down the stairs Olberman asked, "So how's the sleuthing going, inspector? Have you determined who poisoned the port?"

"Not yet, sir, but I'm working on it. I'd like to ask you a few questions about what you remember of that night, if I may?"

"Fire away, inspector. I've got nothing to hide."

"Well, I'm trying to establish everyone's movements right after dinner."

"Let's see. I played bridge with Kenji, Wu Lin, and Francois, if I remember right. We played until Fenton came in to tell us that Krieger had been found. It was Kenji and Wu Lin partnered against me and the Frenchy. They beat us pretty badly, too. Never play cards with inscrutable orientals, inspector."

"Did you go directly to the lounge at the end of dinner?"

"Not anyplace else to go, is there?" Olberman said. "Oh, I get you. No, I made a stop in the restroom. A man's got to pee, you know, after those boring dinners. Practically everyone does. I think Kenji was coming out as I was going in. You can ask him."

"I will, sir," McKernan commented. "Did you happen to pass through the bar area on your way to or from the restroom?"

"I don't know. I guess I must have. It's the shortest path."

"While you did so, you didn't happen to notice the glass of port on the bar, did you?"

"Can't say that I did, inspector. Can't stand the stuff myself. Too sweet. Give me a shot of bourbon any day."

"Did you know Mr. Krieger at all, Mr. Olberman?"

"No. Can't say that I did, other than seeing him around the club. He wasn't very sociable, if you know what I mean. Didn't play cards or pool or have a drink in the bar with the rest of us. Even your buddy McAndrews won't refuse the occasional drink. But Krieger, he'd just go up to the Cupola and smoke his damned cigars rather than associate with anyone."

"So you didn't know him from Earth? I mean, the two of you were in the same line of business."

"No, never met him before I came up to this god-forsaken planet."

"I see," the inspector said, taking a sip of his drink. He noticed that Olberman had finished his and was looking towards the stairway impatient for Teague's return.

"You wouldn't happen to have any ideas yourself, sir, on who might have wanted to murder Mr. Krieger?"

Olberman turned to look at the inspector with a bloodshot eye.

"Who, me? Why would you ask me that?"

"Oh, no reason, sir. I just thought you might have seen or heard something. Just in passing."

He seemed to think that over for a minute.

"Well, there's Teague, for one. Krieger was always calling him a 'bloody kafir.' Accused him of stealing some of his precious port once. Wasn't Teague's fault at all. Turned out a bottle had been broken in transit. Don't get me wrong, inspector. Teague's all right. Anyhow, it doesn't pay to go around insulting the help. Especially bartenders. Might end up watering your drinks. I always make a point of being polite."

"Yes, I see," McKernan said.

"Then there's Fenton. He and Krieger had a big argument about something in Fenton's office once. Don't know what it was all about, but I could hear them going at it through the wall. When I saw Fenton afterwards, his face was white as a sheet."

"Did he have problems with the rest of the staff?"

"Not that I know of. Of course I don't hobnob with the help. I don't think the chef cared for him much, but I never could figure out why."

"Chef Duro?"

"Yeah. The chef comes up during dinner sometimes. Asks people how they liked their food. But he never asked Krieger. You notice things like that."

"Did he ever complain about Jeeves?"

"The butler? That cold fish? No, Krieger got along with him just fine."

Olberman didn't seem inclined to say anything more. Finally McKernan asked, "What about the members? Did Krieger have any conflicts with them?"

"Well, Krieger didn't seem too fond of Wu Lin. Probably because he's Chinese. Kenji, too, for that matter. The rest of us he didn't seem to mind. I guess we were white enough for him. Don't get me wrong. I like Kenji. He's a great guy. Better than Boris, certainly. That one's too Russian if you ask me."

McKernan decided not to.

Olberman had drained his glass and was sucking on an ice cube. Teague hadn't returned yet from his trip to the cellar. Finally, Olberman gave up and stood up a little unsteadily.

"Well, inspector, unless you want to continue the third degree here, I've got to get ready for dinner."

"No. I think you've answered all my questions for the moment. Thank you sir, for your help."

A minute later, Teague returned carrying several bottles. "Is he gone, inspector?"

"Yes, I think he went up to his room."

"Just as well. Don't get me wrong, inspector, Mr. Olberman is a friendly guy. But sometimes he drinks too much. That's one should never 've come to Mars, if you get me."

"It gets to some people that way," McKernan said. There certainly had been times when he'd first come to Mars when he'd drunk more than was good for him.

"Can I pour you another, inspector?"

"No, it's time I should get back to work.   Thanks, anyway."

He was about to leave the bar when his communicator sounded. A check of the ID showed it was Ferris.

"What is it, constable?" McKernan said, walking over to one of the chairs towards the rear of the bar.

"I've heard from my friend on Earth," Ferris answered.

"That was quick," McKernan said, especially considering the delay in communications between the two planets, he added mentally.

"I told you he was good."

"So what did he find?"

"Well, my friend's pretty good with Spanish. He found an old gossip column out of Montevideo. About fifteen years old. It implied that the wife of one Leo Kichler, an up and coming mining executive was having an affair with a Peter Krieger. Seems Krieger was hitting the local social scene back then flashing a lot of money around. He was seen escorting Maria Kichler around to some of the clubs while her husband was away on business. Nothing seems to have come of it though. The Kichlers are still married."

"That's interesting," the inspector commented. "Anything else?"

"Not so far. He said he'd keep digging."

"Good. And good work, too, for recommending him, Ferris.   Let him know that we'll be showing our appreciation."

"I'll do that, sir."

Another complication the inspector thought to himself, after Ferris had disconnected. But did an affair fifteen years earlier provide enough of a motive for murder, particularly if it was only a rumor?   Or was he just looking for something to divert his attention from McAndrews?

CHAPTER 19
THE DOCTOR'S SECRET

McKernan looked at the time. It was 1800. He had told Beth that he'd be home in time for dinner. Given the current state of their relationship, he'd rather not have to cancel. Besides it had been a long day, perhaps too long. The interviews with the remaining members could wait until tomorrow. Sunday might give him a better chance of catching them, in any case. Mars might operate on a seven day a week basis, but administrative functions still tended to be suspended on Sunday.

Elisabeth was preparing dinner when the inspector arrived home at their hut in Hut Town. The doctor had had little experience with cooking before coming to Mars, but she did try to pull her weight in the culinary department, especially when her shift schedule and the press of McKernan's duties meant she arrived home first.

Cooking on Mars certainly presented a host of challenges. Meat of any kind and dairy were expensive and often hard to come by as they had to for the most part be imported from Earth. Vegetables, particularly those that could be grown in small spaces were much more plentiful, but spices and herbs were largely limited to those one grew oneself or which could be bartered or traded amongst acquaintances. A small collection of pots and planters at the back of the hut provided much of what ended up on their table. Even the methods of cooking had to be tailored to the environment. The air pressure in the hut, and in most of the sealed habitations on Mars was kept low by

Earth standards lowering the boiling point of water to the point of requiring the use of pressure cookers for many more dishes than would have been the norm on Earth. The three electric burner cooktop that McKernan had acquired was an extravagance by Martian standards. Still, most Martians tried to eat as well as they could afford as a means of coping with the hostile environment.

"Care for a drink?" McKernan asked after removing his pistol and placing it on the small table next to the airlock.

"Love one!" the doctor answered, looking up from where she was chopping peppers.

As McKernan poured two glasses of "whiskey" over ice, he felt guilty. The last few days at the Mars Club he'd been drinking spirits that would have been expensive even on Earth. The "whiskey" he had just poured was really just alcohol fermented from whatever was available and adulterated with flavorings and food coloring to present a simulation of the Earth product. Distinctions as to Bourbon, rye or Scotch were largely irrelevant. The carbonation provided by the splash of soda wouldn't last long in the low air pressure, either. Still, it was alcohol.

He set Elisabeth's drink on the counter where she was working and took a sip of his own.

"How's the Case of the Poisoned Port going?"

"Slowly. As far as I can determine, everyone who was in the Club that night had the opportunity to put the cyanide in the port. The glass was sitting on the bar for ten minutes or so, and during that time every single one of them was out of the sight of everyone else for at least a couple of minutes. No one has even a hint of an alibi, though none of them were doing anything out of the ordinary or unexpected during the time the glass was waiting on the bar."

"What about the butler?" the doctor asked impishly.

"Jeeves? What about him?"

"Well, isn't it always the butler that did it? I mean in mysteries? And don't tell me his name is really Jeeves?"

"No, his name is actually William Watson. Calling him Jeeves is just sort of a joke. He doesn't seem to mind. As to the butler being a culprit, that's largely a myth. The butler rarely was featured as the criminal in classic mysteries. I looked it up."

"Tell me you didn't," Elisabeth protested.

"You can find the strangest things in the cloud."

"Well if the butler didn't do it, who did?"

"I didn't say the butler didn't do it. He and the barman, Teague, probably had the best chance of dropping the cyanide in the port without being detected. The problem is, I haven't found a motive for either one of them."

"So, where does that leave you?"

"Good question. The victim might not have been particularly likable, but he didn't seem to have interacted enough with anyone to have made an enemy. At least since he's been on Mars. There's nothing much to discover in his past, at least his official past, to think it might be a reason for murder. Except for some gossip, that is."

"Ooh. Tell me. I love gossip. There's not enough of it on Mars."

"Well it seems there were rumors about an affair between Krieger and Leo Kichler's wife some fifteen years back. Kichler is the local head of Rio Plata and was at the dinner, so he's on the list of suspects."

"What did he say when you asked him about the affair?"

"I haven't had the chance yet. I was tied up most of the day interviewing the staff and meeting with the governor."

"Tsangambo? That must have been interesting. How did that go?"

"Surprisingly well, considering. After some initial sparing he was actually quite open. He has his own theories and made a remarkable claim about Krieger."

"Some mysterious secret from his past?" the doctor quipped.

"That's actually beginning to look more likely," McKernan said, suddenly serious. "As far as the record goes, Mr. Krieger might as well not have existed before fifteen years ago. Greenwood said that he'd had cosmetic surgery at some point back then, apparently to change his appearance. Maybe he *was* hiding something in his past. The governor, at least, seemed to be hinting at that."

"And the governor was at the dinner," Beth said. "A coincidence?"

"He's an honorary member of the club. He claims that he goes there just because the food is good. Personally, I think he attends just to tweak the noses of the capitalists that *are* members."

"Well, what is this secret that he hint at?"

"He spun me a story dating back to the Rhodesian War. About a rebel unit called 17 Commando that committed all sorts of atrocities during the course of the war. At the end of the conflict they disappeared, allegedly with a fortune in diamonds they had looted. Tsangambo claimed that someone he knew thought that Krieger had been one of the leaders of 17 Commando."

"What do *you* think?"

"Of course the story is complete hearsay, and second hand hearsay at that but he suggested that I ask Otis about it."

"Otis? Otis McAndrews? But he's such a nice old man. Surely the governor wasn't insinuating that he was involved?"

"He refused to elaborate further, only suggesting that I ask McAndrews himself. I got the feeling that he had realized he had maybe said more than he should have."

"So, have you asked McAndrews about it?"

"I haven't had the chance yet. The curious thing is that when I asked Otis last night if he'd ever run across Krieger during his time in Africa he became evasive."

"Evasive? That doesn't sound like McAndrews at all. He's always struck me as being so honest and straight forward."

"Yes. That's just what has me bothered. Otis can keep a secret well enough, but he's never lied to me."

"You can't seriously think that he's your murderer, can you?"

"Right now, I don't know what to think."

"I think you should forget about it for the moment, at least during dinner."

Later, after dinner, while they were still sitting at the table Elisabeth said, "There's something I have to tell you, Erik."

"What's that?" McKernan asked, feeling certain from her tone that he wasn't going to like what he heard.

"I've applied for a job. Back on Earth. They are opening a recuperation facility for people returning from long periods in space or on other planets. They are looking for people who've had personal experience with what conditions off Earth are like."

"I see. When was this?" McKernan asked flatly.

"Three months ago," the doctor replied.

"And you're just mentioning it now?"

"I didn't think I had much of a shot at getting the position. Knowing how you'd react, I didn't see any point in bringing it up. But a few days ago I got a confirmation that I'm one of the finalists."

McKernan sat silently.

"You have to understand, Erik. The end of my contract on Mars is coming up soon. I have to look for a new position. This seemed like the best opportunity for me."

"I'm sure they'd renew your contract at the hospital."

"Yes, they probably would. Greenwood has said as much. But I'm not sure I want to remain on Mars, Erik. Not for another three years. That would mean being gone from Earth for six years. You know yourself that after that long a time going back may not be a possibility. Even if it's still feasible physically, being away from Earth that long, there may be nothing to go back to."

"And us? What about us?"

"This isn't about us, Erik. It's about me. You've made yourself a place here on Mars. You're part of the bloody planet. I'm not, and I'm not sure that I want to be. Don't misunderstand me, it's not that I don't love you. I just don't know if I can stand spending the rest of my life inside a tin can. Never going outside. Never feeling the wind and the rain and the sun on my face. Can you understand that, Erik? Can you?"

"I understand. I'm sorry, Beth. I really am."

"I know, Erik. And so am I. And I won't ask you to come back to Earth with me. I know you've made your choice, and I respect that, it's just that I haven't made it mine. It's no one's fault. It's just the way it is."

"When will you know for certain?"

"They said that I'd know in a couple of days if I've been selected."

"And if you're not? What then? What will you do?"

"I really don't know."

CHAPTER 20
OTIS'S AFRICAN ADVENTURE

McKernan gave Ferris Sunday off. It was unlikely any of his enquiries into missing cyanide would be looked into until Monday morning, and there would be more than enough for the constable to do in the upcoming week. The inspector, however, would not spend his Sunday relaxing. He thought it might well be his best chance to catch the club members for interviews. He also thought he might get the best results if he talked to them without the constable being present.

During the course of the afternoon, he was able to complete the questioning of most of the members. To McKernan's annoyance, Kichler had chosen to go off to one of Rio Plata's mining operations and was not available. While the inspector had not given explicit directions not to leave Mars City, on Mars such instructions were superfluous as spaceship departures were limited and well known, but it was inconvenient.

At the end of the interview sessions McKernan found himself standing at the bar with a whiskey and soda on the bar wondering if he really wanted to go home. Finishing his drink he left the bar and took a quick peek into the lounge to see if any of the other members that he wanted to interview were around.

The only one in the room was Otis McAndrews who was sitting in a chair apparently going over some reports. In light of the governor's veiled comment, sooner or later

McKernan would have to confront his friend. He might as well get it out of the way.

"Do you mind if I disturb you for a moment, sir?" the inspector asked.

McAndrews looked up with a smile on his face. Setting aside his papers he responded, "Not at all, Erik. Please have a seat. How goes the investigation?"

"Slowly, I'm afraid. Plenty of people seem to have had an opportunity, but so far I haven't been able to establish any sort of a motive. I did have an interesting conversation with the governor, though."

"Oh?" McAndrews said with a note of curious skepticism. "I have a hard time imagining our beloved governor revealing anything. Unless it would further his own agenda, that is. I'd be careful around Tsangambo, Erik. He's one of the faction in the U.N. that is opposed to any sort of home rule for Mars. They'd like nothing more than to stir trouble up here."

"I've learned never to take anyone at face value, sir," McKernan said flatly. "Still, I'm not sure how a murder investigation on Mars could be an influence on interplanetary politics."

"Tsangambo and his ilk tend to view everything through the filter of Africa's colonial past. His feelings about capitalism and the white man are almost pathological. If he could link the head of one of the corporations to that past, particularly if there were a scandal involved, it would be a powerful argument for his side in the negotiations."

"I'm afraid that he's already trying to make that connection with Krieger. He claimed, though he said he had no proof of it, that Krieger had been part of something called 17 Commando during the Rhodesian War," McKernan said watching his friend closely. He thought he detected a hint of a shudder before McAndrews face resumed its implacable aspect.

"The Rhodesian War was a nasty business, Erik. It left scars on a lot of people, not all of them physical."

"The governor also seemed to think that you knew something about it. Is there something that you haven't told me, Otis?"

The look McAndrews gave the inspector was one of profound sadness.

"You have to understand, Erik, that I didn't mention anything when you asked before because I didn't think it was relevant."

"I think now, perhaps, is the time for you to tell me, sir," McKernan said softly.

"Yes, perhaps it is. It's something of a long story."

"I've got the time, sir," McKernan said.

"I was in Africa at the time the Rhodesian War flared up. I was working at my first job out of university. I was with Anglo-African Mining at the time. That's a predecessor of Anglo-Martian. I and a couple of other engineers were doing a survey of a mining concession Anglo-African had gotten along the Kwando River. That's along the border of Zimbabwe and Angola. We were working on the Zimbabwe side.

"You have to understand that that part of Africa had been pretty much a basket case since the end of the twentieth century. Mugabe and his cronies had made such a complete mess of the economy, that the country has never really recovered. The government of Zimbabwe had granted Anglo-African a mining concession in the hopes of improving the situation. Provide jobs, boost the currency reserves, earn foreign exchange credits, that sort of thing. We had the full support of and assistance of the government.

"As I said, I along with a couple of others and a group of local workers were doing the preliminary survey to determine the best location for the mine and processing plant. There was another man, Wilson, fresh out of university like myself, and our boss, O'Rourke, a geologist in his forties. Things were going along quite well. It was really very pleasant, more of a camping trip than work. We treated the local crew well and they were all happy to have the work and get paid in real money. O'Rourke was an old Africa hand and knew how to get along well with his men.

"Everything was going well until the war flared up. To this day, the origins of the whole thing are pretty mysterious. As far as anyone knows, a bunch of white mercenaries, most of whom appeared to be Afrikaaners managed to put together a rag-tag army of white mercenaries from around Africa along with some locals from one of the tribes that had been getting the shaft for the last century. It really wasn't much more than a guerilla force, but then the government army wasn't much either. The army was pretty corrupt and mostly armed with fifty year old gear that was falling apart.

"The rebels overran most of the western half of the country in a matter of weeks. The government forces managed to make a stand around Lusaka and things degenerated into a stalemate for a while, with neither side strong enough to overpower the other. After that it all dissolved into a series of raids and counter raids by small parties. 17 Commando was one of those groups fighting on the rebel side, though after a few months they seemed to be fighting more for themselves than anyone else.

"We got caught in the middle of things pretty early on. They came down on our camp with about fifty men armed with AK-47's and a couple of truck mounted anti-aircraft guns. We didn't stand a chance. We had a pair of hunting rifles and that was it. They killed all of the locals in the crew that didn't manage to escape into the bush. O'Rourke was shot dead almost at the first. I took a bullet to the leg and one to the shoulder. Wilson might have been able to escape, but he tried to patch me up instead.

"We were both taken prisoner, Wilson and I. They took us back to their camp. Wilson tried to take care of my wounds as best he could, but he wasn't a medical man and there wasn't much in the way of supplies. The rebels had a man they called a doctor, but he was drunk most of the time."

"I take it that the group that captured you was 17 Commando?"

"That's what we found out later. You have to understand, that I was delirious most of this time. I have only vague recollections of most of what happened. I never talked with any of the leaders. They interrogated Wilson a few times, but they soon figured out neither one of us knew anything useful to them.

"A few months after the start of the war the U.N. and the African Union got their act together and the African Union sent in some troops. At first, they were just there to shore up the defenses around Lusaka, but eventually they started to go after the rebels in the west.

"The group we were with started to be hard pressed. We moved around quite a bit. I think we crossed over the river a couple of times into Angola, but I couldn't swear to it. As I said, I was in a pretty bad way. I don't think I would have pulled through if it hadn't been for Wilson's nursing.

"They tell me we were held as captives for eight months. The group we were with kept getting smaller. Most of the local Africans that were in the group melted away in the night, leaving just the white mercenaries. From what Wilson told me in my lucid periods they weren't much more than a bandit gang towards the end, more interested in collecting portable loot than achieving anything political.

"Finally, there came a showdown. The A.U. troops cornered our bunch. Had them mostly surrounded. There were only about a dozen left, and a couple of those were wounded. I suppose they could have surrendered, but they didn't. That's when they shot Wilson. Made him kneel on the ground and put a bullet into the back of his head. Then they shot their own wounded. I don't know why they didn't do the same to me. Perhaps they thought that I was dead already.

"The next thing I know, I'm in a hospital in Lusaka and they're getting me ready to be airlifted back to Britain. The doctor at the hospital said he couldn't understand how I could still be alive. They said the same thing at the hospital in London.

"It took me six months in the hospital to recover my strength, and another half year before I was back to anything like my old self. It was a pretty terrible experience. You can see why I never talk about it, can't you?"

McKernan only nodded. He had had his own experiences with guerilla warfare in Burma and Paraguay during his time in the military.

"Just where does Peter Krieger fit in with all this, Otis?"

"I honestly don't know. You have to remember I was out of it most of those eight months of captivity. It all seems a bad dream. And I never did get close to any of the officers. I only saw them at a distance."

"But you had your suspicions?"

"Yes. There was one man, the leader. It was his voice more than anything. The first time I heard Krieger, it sent a chill down my spine. I thought it was the same voice. But I could easily have been mistaken. It was a long time ago, Erik. I was sick. It could be I was fooled by the accent.

Krieger doesn't look much like the 17 Commando leader that I remember, but then that was twenty some years ago and that man had a big bushy beard. It might have been the same man, but it might as easily have not. Do you understand?"

McKernan did. He knew that eye witness accounts were remarkably unreliable, particularly with unfamiliar faces.

"So you chose not to tell anyone about your suspicions?"

"What else could I have done? If I had been even half-way certain that Krieger was the man responsible for the death of Wilson, the man who saved my life, don't you think I would have done something. But I wasn't. I still am not. And given the possible repercussions, that I might well be accusing an innocent man, I chose to remain silent."

"I'm not blaming you, Otis," McKernan said gently. "I might well have done the same thing were I in your place." After a moment he asked, "Is Tsangambo aware of your experiences?"

"I suspect he's read the official A.U. report. It's public knowledge. There were war crimes trials held for some of the rebels. And I'm sure it's the kind of thing he'd be interested in if only to use for political advantage."

"What happened to the men of 17 Commando, Otis? Were they ever caught?"

"None of the leaders were. They all disappeared at the end of the war. As I said, towards the end they had been more interested in loot than the war. I remember something Wilson said a few days before he was killed. He said that he'd seen a big pile of diamonds being divided up amongst the leaders. He made it sound as if each of them were carrying several million dollars apiece in uncut stones. More than enough to help someone get away."

"Or to start a mining company in South America," the inspector commented dryly.

"Or to start a company in South America," McAndrews echoed.

"Does anyone else know about your suspicions?"

"I don't think so, Erik," McAndrews replied. "You're the first person I've spoken to about the whole business in nearly twenty years."

"I want to thank you, Otis, for telling me. I don't know if it has any bearing on the case. We still don't know if Krieger really even was with 17 Commando. But it *is* possible someone thought he was and chose to act upon that belief. I'm still operating on the premise that Krieger was murdered for something in his past."

"I'd appreciate it if you didn't spread this story around unless you become certain about Krieger," McAndrews cautioned. "Tsangambo would like nothing more than to link Krieger to 17 Commando. It wouldn't even have to be true. People like that aren't concerned with the truth, Erik." There was a note of desperation in his voice.

"But I am, Otis," McKernan said. "And I will get to it sooner or later."

Taking a look at the clock on the wall he said, "It's getting late. I should be going. And don't worry, I'll keep this between you and me for the time being."

As he walked home, McKernan wondered how much of the truth McAndrews had told him.

CHAPTER 21
NEWS FROM EARTH

On Monday morning, McKernan's first stop was at the police station. Gaeretts was manning the front desk as usual. The sergeant was an old Mars hand who had been the departments first hire. He had been the one that had shown McKernan the ropes. Now he handled most of the department's day to day operations, though he was still available for backup when needed. He could be a handy man to have on your side in a fight.

"Anything I need to know about?" McKernan asked as he passed the desk into the back of the station.

"No, it was a pretty slow night Saturday, and Sunday was even quieter. We've got four sleeping it off in the drunk tank, two in the holding cells for fighting. I had to take one guy to the hospital to get stitched up. He got cut by a knife at Thelma's. The one who did it is one of the ones in the holding cells."

McKernan just nodded. From Gaeretts' report it had been a fairly typical weekend. Most of the crime his small department had to deal with involved miners and construction workers in town for a couple of days rest and recreation. They'd drink too much, maybe bust up some property, sometimes each other. Occasionally someone would take his frustrations out on one of the working girls out at the far end of Hut Town, but that was rare. With men outnumbering women seven to one, even the prostitutes had a certain amount of respect and protection. Drunks were mostly allowed to sleep it off. The disorderly were fined and the event was noted on their employment records. The serious offenders were held until they could be shipped back to Earth. Mars had no judges, no trials, no prison system, just the fiat of the Trust Authority.

Really serious crime was rare on Mars. Most of the sociopaths and career criminals were weeded out by the psychological evaluation everyone had to go through before being allowed to land on the planet. Given the expense of transporting someone to Mars and the resources it took to support them once they got there, the corporations were more than happy with the procedure. That didn't eliminate crime, but it kept it down. Still, Mars was a high stress environment with people cooped up in small spaces for long periods of time. A few of them snapped, sometimes tragically. And given that nearly everyone had come to Mars for the money it was expected that the temptation to get rich quickly would tempt some to cross the line.

With only a few dozen constables to cover the entire planet, claim jumping posed an ever present problem. So did theft of supplies in the out there. Sometimes the disputes ended in death. It was easy to think you could get away with something when there were thousands of square kilometers in which to hide bodies. Usually, it was all too clear, though, who the culprits were. There had, however, been a few murders that McKernan had had to solve in his years on Mars. Not many, but a few.

The inspector went on through the bull-pen to the small space in the rear of the station that was his office. It wasn't much, but he didn't complain. When he had first come to Mars, the station had still been housed in one of the old inflatable huts, a thin skin of aluminum and a few centimeters of sprayed on insulation the only protection against the harsh Martian environment where the air pressure was nil and the temperature rarely reached freezing.

He was checking his e-mails on his computer when Ferris poked his head through the door.

"Have we had any responses yet to our enquiries?" McKernan asked.

"Not yet," Ferris answered, "but I did get some more info from that friend of mine I mentioned. I forwarded it to you. There are a couple of interesting items that he turned up."

"Like what?"

"It seems that there was the hint of a scandal at a well known men's club in London a few years back. Something about allegations of club accounts being fudged. The case was never prosecuted."

"And this is noteworthy why?"

"It turns out that the club steward at the time was one Howard Fenton. As I said, no charges were filed, but Fenton resigned his position. He didn't work again until he took the job with the Mars Club."

"Seems we may have a few things to ask Mr. Fenton," McKernan said. He outlined Olberman's report of an argument between Fenton and Krieger. "You're friend has been busy. And productive. Anything else?"

"Not much, I'm afraid. He couldn't find anything of note on any of the other members. Nothing unusual turned up on the butler, Duckworth, or Teague, either. The chef, Duro, was clean, but it turns out he had an older brother. He was a chef, too, working at a resort in Angola. It was somewhere along the border with Zimbabwe. He was killed in a cross border raid by some rebel group."

"When was this?" asked, suddenly alert.

"Quite some time ago. During the Rhodesian War. Jose Duro must have been just a kid. The news story mentioned something about 17 Commando. Odd coincidence about that. My friend also dug up a story about Otis McAndrews. He was abducted and held prisoner by 17 Commando about the same time."

"Yes, he told me the story last night," McKernan said thoughtfully.

"Think it means anything?" Ferris asked eagerly.

"I doubt if there's any connection between McAndrews and Duro. I'm not as sure about Krieger. I'd certainly like to know where he was during the Rhodesian War. Did your friend have any luck tracing his past?"

"Not that far back, I'm afraid. Nothing seems to have appeared in the press before he shows up in South America a few years later. When he did appear, there was a lot of speculation in the financial press about who the mysterious Mr. Krieger was. He was already quite wealthy at the time. Oh, speaking of the financial press, there was one other tid-bit my friend unearthed."

"What's that?" the inspector enquired.

"There was a piece about Transamerican Minerals. Mostly background, evaluating their stock, that kind of thing. They seemed to think that the company wasn't exactly broke, but that they could certainly use a big strike. Their last few ventures hadn't proved to be as profitable as they had projected."

"Did it mention anything about Olberman?"

"Not directly, but it did hint that if the company's fortunes didn't improve soon, some of the top executives might find themselves out on the street."

"Now that *is* interesting. I caught Olberman in the bar at the Mars Club Saturday. He'd been drinking quite a bit. Maybe he has a reason to. Let your friend know that I'm very happy with his work. I'll put through a payment authorization. And tell him I might want to use his services again if the occasion arises."

"I'll do that, sir," Ferris said with a smile.

"And while I'm thinking about it, did you turn up anything with your cyanide enquiries?"

"Not yet. But most of the labs agreed to do an inventory of their stock. I should hear back from them later today or tomorrow."

"Good. I think it's time for us to get back to work," McKernan announced. "I had a chance to interview most of the members Sunday who were at the dinner. Why don't you listen to the recordings and tell me if anything strikes you as interesting."

"Sure thing, sir," Ferris said, happy that he was being kept in the loop.

McKernan decided that he might as well review the interviews himself. Nothing in particular had struck him at the time they had been made, but one never knew what might turn up listening to them a second time.

His conversation with the Russian, Boris Kasperovski had been brief and not terribly productive.

"Could you tell me, sir, what you did at the end of dinner?"

"I had some correspondence to work on. A progress report for my bosses back on Earth. I wanted some peace and quiet, so I went to the library. I worked there until Fenton gathered us in the lounge and you made your announcement."

"And you didn't leave the library before that?"

"No."

"We're also trying to fix the order that people left the dining room. I was hoping you might help us with that?"

"Let me think. A few of us talked to the governor for a minute or two, Paying respects, you understand. I think Wu Lin, Gordon, Kichler, maybe one other. Then I went to the library."

"So this was before the governor left?"

"Yes. I saw him walk by the library on his way out, so he must have remained in the dining room after I left."

"Did you know Mr. Krieger at all?"

"No. I'm not that comfortable in English. He was not a friendly man in any case. I knew who he was, of course, but not personally, no."

"Anything else you can think of that might be helpful?"

"I'm afraid not, inspector," which had ended the interview. Other than confirming some of the details of the timeline, it had not been terribly helpful.

Wu Lin of Celestial Minerals had been nearly as terse.

"After dinner I paid my respects to the governor. There were several others doing the same. Gordon, Kichler and a couple of others. We were just standing around, really, trying to be polite. It is not always easy to do with the governor. Then I went to the restroom and after to play bridge in the lounge."

"So you were one of the last to leave the dining room?"

"Yes, I must have been, though there were probably four or five of us that left within a few seconds of each other. After the governor took his leave Gordon and Kichler walked out together. I said a few words to Fenton about a good dinner and then left myself."

"I believe the other bridge players were Fujika, DuChene, and Olberman. They had gone on ahead of you?"

"Yes, DuChene went first to get the cards and things ready. Kenji left soon after that and then Olberman left a little later."

"How was your game, sir?"

"Oh, Kenji and I won handily. DuChene is a solid player, but Olberman is a bit impulsive in his bidding, particularly when he's had too much drink." There was a hint of disapproval in his voice. "I would prefer to play with someone else, but the pool of players is limited. McAndrews is a good if somewhat conventional player, but he said he wasn't up to it. Olberman asked to play and there really wasn't any way to refuse."

"If I might ask, do you play for high stakes?"

"Not particularly. A dollar a point I think. Most of the players in the club are pretty evenly matched, so it evens out over time."

"And Mr. Olberman—?"

"I'd say he tends to lose more than he wins."

"Did Mr. Krieger ever play?"

"No, Mr. Krieger never played games, not bridge, not billiards, not chess. And he didn't like to associate with non-Caucasians, inspector," Wu Lin said with distaste.

"Did you have that kind of problem with any of the other members?"

"No," Wu Lin replied with a laugh. "We are all men of business far from home. Whatever we think in private, we are all too well behaved to let it show."

"Even Mr. Olberman?"

"Mr. Olberman is too much the American, inspector. He just wants to be liked."

That comment had essentially terminated the interview.

Gordon had been off at a mining camp for the day and the interview had been conducted by satellite which had kept it both brief and choppy as the inevitable relay delay added time between questions and answers. Not that he had added much. He and Kichler had been in the group talking to the governor. They had left the dining room together. Kichler had stopped at the restroom while he had gone ahead. He was still choosing a cue when Kichler showed up. They had played until Fenton asked them to come to the lounge. Jeeves had been in to take drink orders, brandy for Kichler, rye for himself. He had thought Krieger standoffish. Kichler seemed to have a strong antipathy against the man for some unspoken reason. Other than that the club members tended to be polite but reserved with the South African.

DuChene, when he was interviewed, had been charming in a French sort of way, but not particularly helpful.

"I think I was the first to leave after Krieger. I told Kenji and Wu Lin that I'd get things ready. I was going to order a drink from Teague, but he wasn't behind the bar, so I went ahead to the lounge to get out the cards and the things for scoring. I knew Jeeves would be in to ask about drinks, anyway, so it wasn't urgent. Kenji came into the lounge next, then Stan and Wu Lin. We played, not well. Stan was a bit too aggressive in his bidding. Then Fenton called everyone together. That was the first I realized anything was wrong."

As to Krieger:

"I didn't really know him. I tried to have a conversation about South Africa one, I have a friend who lives there, but he was very, how you say, reserved. After that I gave up. There are more congenial people to talk to. Of course I dealt with him on business, but it was always very professional."

As for Nordlund, he had been affable but had not very helpful. The gist of his interview was that he had hung around the dining room for a minute or so, noticed Stan Olberman hurrying off with some urgency, presumably to the restroom. He had thought that a good idea, waited a decent interval to give Olberman time to conduct his business, and then followed. When he was done, he went into the lounge where he sat reading. He had exchanged a few pleasantries with McAndrews, but that was all. He had realized that something was up when Fenton came to fetch McAndrews, but hadn't known what until the inspector had made his announcement.

In regards to Krieger, Nordlund "always tried to be on polite terms with customers." Other than that he had no knowledge or opinions about the South African.

As a clue to the murderer, the interviews were singularly unhelpful, McKernan thought. All the testimony seemed to fit with the timeline he and Ferris had constructed. There were no inconsistencies which might serve as a trap for the murderer. On the other hand, each of the members had or could have passed through the bar area without being observed for the few seconds it would have taken to poison the port.

He still had not had the opportunity to question Leo Kichler, but he had a feeling that the results would just be more of the same.

CHAPTER 22
FENTON CONFESSES

After reviewing the interview recordings, McKernan felt the need for some action. It was now the third day after the murder and he hadn't really made any progress in narrowing down the list of suspects. It was time to shake things up a bit. He got up from his desk and went out into the bull-pen where Ferris was sitting at a desk.

"Have you finished listening to the interviews, constable?"

"Yes, sir," Ferris replied.

"Good. Then I think it's time that we had our chat with Mr. Fenton."

Fenton had provided the inspector with a pass card which eliminated the need to press the buzzer and have someone on the inside let them into the club. McKernan took advantage of that and Ferris and he passed through the airlock and into the vestibule. Somewhat to his surprise, the club steward was standing behind the front desk when they entered apparently attending to some paperwork.

"Good afternoon, inspector," Fenton remarked as he looked up to see who had entered the club. "Still hard at it, I see."

"Yes, and I'm afraid we will be until this business is resolved."

"Well, if there is anything I can do to be of assistance—" Fenton said in his most professional manner.

"As a matter of fact there is, Mr. Fenton. Several things have come to light which I would like to discuss with you."

"Yes?"

"Perhaps we could go someplace more private?"

"Would my office be acceptable? Or would you prefer to give me the third degree in the interrogation room?" Fenton asked somewhat flippantly.

"I think your office would be adequate," Mckernan replied without humor.

The door to the steward's office was located directly behind the front desk. Fenton opened it and motioned them inside. It was not a large room, a little over two meters wide and perhaps five meters long. Visualizing the floor plan of the club, McKernan knew the bar was just the other side of the wall. Some might have found the space cozy; the inspector just found it cramped. At one end of the office was a desk with a monitor and keyboard. A photo in a silver frame of an elderly couple, presumably Fenton's parents sat next to the computer monitor. At the other end there was a clothes rack from which hung a number of white waiter's jackets and suit coats. A file cabinet and shelving took up most of the rest of the floor space. Several travel posters of tropical beech scenes filled the available wall space.

"I'm afraid I only have the two chairs, inspector," Fenton said apologetically.

"I can stand, sir," Constable Ferris said in response.

"Hopefully this won't take long," McKernan said.

"What is it you wished to ask me, inspector?" Fenton asked.

"I had an interesting conversation with Mr. Olberman on Saturday. He mentioned an incident in which he overheard an argument between yourself and Mr. Krieger."

"Mr. Olberman has a habit of saying a bit too much when he's been drinking, which is much of the time." Fenton's careful diction had slipped a little, betraying his London roots.

"Still, did such an argument take place? And if so, what was the nature of the argument?"

"I admit Mr. Krieger and I did have words, inspector. It was over one of his bloody bottles of port. It had been broken in transit. Teague reported it to me as soon as he opened the case. I have the pictures that I took for the damage claim against Interplanetary. I can show you those if you'd like."

"That might be helpful."

Fenton played around with his keyboard for a moment. An image appeared on the monitor screen. It showed a top view of a case of port bottles. Sadly, one of the corner bottles did appear to have suffered damage, the red liquid having soaked into the packing material around the bottle.

"And here's the claim form I filed," Fenton said. A quick look at the form convinced McKernan that it was legitimate and that the date matched Olberman's story.

"I take it Krieger wasn't satisfied?"

"No. He was quite unreasonable about the whole matter. He blamed Teague. Accused him of faking the damage to steal the bottle. He was yelling at him in the bar. I asked him into my office to talk it over. When he did, he said he wanted Teague to be fired for incompetence. Well, it wasn't Teague's fault at all. I told him that I had filed a claim and that in due course Interplanetary Transport would undoubtedly issue a check and he would be reimbursed for the cost of the bottle on Earth and one twelfth of the shipping cost."

"That certainly sounds reasonable," McKernan commented.

"Not for Mr. Krieger. He wanted me to pay for the whole bloody case immediately. I said I couldn't do that. The funds would have had to come out of my own account. The port was expensive enough, but you know what shipping costs are like, inspector. I said that as soon as the claim was processed he would be reimbursed. He called me a cheat and a crook. Said he knew all about me. About why I was on Mars. I'm afraid that's when I lost my temper."

"I see," McKernan said, not without sympathy. "That does bring up another point, Mr. Fenton. In going over your records, I've notice a lapse in your employment history. There's a period of some nine months when you were unemployed. Would you care to comment?"

Fenton sighed. "I suppose that it was bound to come up sooner or later. I might as well tell you my side of the story."

"I would appreciate that."

"I was steward at a club in London. Not one of the big ones, but it had been around a few centuries. It was a good position. Perfectly respectable. The pay could have been better, but given what the job situation on Earth is like, I had no complaints. I'd been there for a couple of years and everything was going along swimmingly.   Then some discrepancies came up in the accounts. Turns out the chef and the wine steward had both been fiddling their budgets. I probably should have caught on, but I was a trusting soul. I had known them both for some time. I had had no part of the fiddling, and the club wanted to avoid a scandal, so I was allowed to resign. No charges were filed against the other two, either.

"Well, after that I tried to get another job, but no one would take me on. Not that the club torpedoed me directly. If anyone checked my references, they'd say that it was policy to only give out employment dates. Which they did.

But rumors got around all the same. Things are bad enough with jobs as it is. No one was going to risk hiring a steward with a taint. It tried for other kinds of jobs. Hotels and such. No luck. Then an advertisement for this job came up. Well, no one in my line wants to go to a place like Mars, no matter what the job pays. But I was desperate by that time. I figured three years working here and I might be able to get something back on Earth. And I have to admit that the pay isn't at all bad. As it was, I think I was the only one with the right kind of experience that applied."

"And if Krieger had reported what he knew?"

"Mr. McAndrews knows all about what happened with my last job. He's no fool. They had a detective agency check into my background before they hired me. The other members of the board of directors know, too. All Mr. Krieger could have done was embarrass me a bit."

"What was the outcome of your argument with Krieger?"

"Oh, we shouted at each other for a couple of minutes, then he stomped out of my office. I handed him the reimbursement check when it came through and I never heard a word about it from him again."

"He never threatened either you or Teague after that?"

"He never said a word to me. I don't think he did to Teague, either."

"Well, I think that clarifies that, though you should have mentioned it earlier."

"I didn't think it that important, inspector. Some of the gentlemen do get worked up about this or that from time to time. Handling it is all part of the job. Is there anything else you'd like to know?"

"Not at the moment, no. You wouldn't happen to know if Mr. Kichler is in the club at the moment, would you?" McKernan asked.

"I believe he is still out at one of the mining camps, inspector," Fenton replied, his professional veneer restored.

"Too bad. Well, I'll just have to catch him some other time."

"I'll mention it to him when he comes in. And inspector?"

"Yes?"

"I'd appreciate it if you wouldn't mention the circumstances of my leaving my last position. Not *all* of the members know about it."

"If it doesn't prove relevant, I see no reason why it needs to be made public."

"Thank you, inspector. I'll be sure to let Mr. Kichler know you're looking for him."

CHAPTER 23
FINNEGAN'S

"What next, sir?" Ferris asked, once they were in the vestibule.

McKernan looked on his constable with a blank expression for a moment, then his features became more animated.

"What next, constable? Why I feel the need for a drink coming on. But not here. Someplace where a man can think."

"Sir?" Ferris asked in puzzlement.

"Are you coming, Ferris?"

"Yes, sir," he replied and followed the inspector back out through the airlock onto the concourse.

Finnegan's is both a Martian institution and one of the planet's biggest mysteries. Located in what was for Mars, prime real estate, it occupies a space on the main concourse almost directly opposite the Mars Club. It is also the closest thing to an Irish pub within fifty million kilometers.

Finnegan's consists of a long narrow room kept intentionally dark. A genuine mahogany bar runs along one wall of the establishment. Small tables with chairs run down the other wall. There is no sound system blaring music and the video screen at the end of the room is normally only turned on for Sunday afternoon football games, games that are prerecorded and anywhere from a few hours to a week old due to the forty minute difference in length between a Martian and Earth day. Somehow, sometime in the last few years, a battered upright piano had appeared against the wall at the end of the bar. There is also a non-electronic dart board which by convention, was placed inconveniently just outside the door to the men's room. The main attraction of Finnegan's is that it serves honest booze at honest prices, that and the personality of the owner, Finnegan himself.

There is some argument as to which is the greatest mystery, Finnegan's the bar, or Finnegan the man. Somehow, when the permanent part of Mars City was first being built, Finnegan managed to corral a piece of prime real estate on the main concourse. Being Irish, he decided to open a bar. How Finnegan manages to stay in business and pay rent to the Trust Authority on what appeared to be a modest business with slender margins is part of the mystery. Why he would choose to do so is the other part.

Finnegan is a portly Irishman who looks to be in his sixties. McKernan knew from his file that he had been born in Macroom, a small town in the south of the Republic. Officially he had come to Mars as a consultant to the U.N. Trust Authority about the time the first fused-silica blocks of the city were being laid down. When his contract was up, he had chosen to stay. Most thought it was for his health, a not implausible reason, the lower gravity being a boon to those with heart conditions. Over the years, of course, various other reasons have surfaced, never to be confirmed by Finnegan or anyone else. Some say that he is a half owner of Anglo-Martian who considers the running of a bar a hobby. Others have claimed that he is blackmailing certain parties at the U.N. The most recent rumor to surface is that he had been the lead investigator of the case against the Very Real IRA for the BIE, the Bureau de Investigation Europe, who had been removed to Mars for his own protection. Frankly, McKernan didn't believe any of the rumors.

What he did believe in, was that Finnegan's was one of the few places on the planet where he could truly relax and think.

Finnegan himself, as was almost invariably the case, was behind the bar when the pair of policeman entered. He gave a desultory wave with a hand holding a bar rag and inquired, "What can I get you, inspector?"

"I think a pair of pints for starters." By custom and tradition when a "pint" was ordered in Finnegan's without a qualifier it was assumed to be a pint of Guinness. How or why Finnegan was able to procure this dark elixir on Mars when what usually passed for beer was a homemade product made from local ingredients which all too often did not even include malted barley, was perhaps the third greatest mystery of Mars. Not that there weren't still some difficulties. Maintaining the proper level of carbonation at the lower air pressure common within Martian structures presented a constant challenge. And try as he might, even with the help of some of the best engineering and scientific talent on the planet, even Finnegan had been unable to reproduced the thick creamy head of the Dublin original.

Still, it was real beer, and not just any beer, but stout. Finnegan poured two glasses, continually fiddling with the elaborate tap apparatus for the best results. He managed to produce two glasses that appeared to be mostly foam which he allowed to sit on the bar for several minutes before completing the pour. They might not have passed muster in Dublin, or for that matter Eniscorthy, but McKernan had had worse in Rangoon.

"Your pints, gentlemen," Finnegan said when he was finally satisfied that he had done his best.

"Thanks," McKernan said picking up the pints, and then to Ferris, "let's grab a table."

They took seats at a table against the far wall towards the rear of the bar. Ferris looked suspiciously at the glass McKernan laid in front of him. Ferris was not a regular at Finnegan's which tended to cater towards the longer term residents of the planet. The fact was, the constable was not much of a drinker and most of his contact with saloons came when he was patrolling the wilder establishments out at the far end of Hut Town.

"Slange," McKernan said as he took the first sip of his beer.

"If you say so, sir," Ferris replied gingerly taking a sip from his own glass.

"You're probably wondering why I dragged you in here, Ferris," McKernan said.

"Well, I was wondering, sir," Ferris responded.

"What I felt was needed was some thinking out loud in private. Away from that stuffy establishment across the way."

"Yes, sir."

"Loosen up, Ferris. Nothing you say will be held against you. I'm interested in your ideas of this case. Frankly, I've kind of reached a limit in my own mind and could do with a fresh point of view. So what do you think about the murder?"

Ferris took a minute to put his thoughts in order, then, after taking another sip from his pint, this one less tentative began to state his case:

"Well, sir, to begin with, we've pretty much established that everyone present that night could have put the cyanide in the port without being spotted. For some, like Teague and the butler, it would have been easier, and for some, like

Mrs. Simpson, it would have been harder, but any one of them *could* have done it."

"You've expressed that point very succinctly, constable, and unfortunately quite accurately. Continue."

"If we can't rule out any one from having access to the port, the next thing to look at I would think would be motive."

"And—"

"Well, that's where it kind of breaks down, sir. If we look at the staff, most of them don't seem to have any connection to Krieger at all. I mean that outside of Teague and Fenton and Jeeves, they hardly seem to have dealt with him."

"What about those three, though?"

"There doesn't seem to be anything to point at Jeeves."

"So the butler didn't do it?" McKernan interrupted.

"Not that we know of, sir," Ferris said trying to remain professional. "Krieger might have had an argument with Teague, but Teague is a bartender. He's got to be use to the occasional belligerent customer."

"Krieger did try to get him fired."

"But we're not even sure that Teague knew about that. I can't see Fenton bringing it up, particularly when he had had his own argument with Krieger about the same thing."

"What about Fenton, then?"

"Same thing. I've got to think that Mr. Fenton is pretty thick-skinned after all the years in his line of work. Of course, it might be a good idea to check with Mr. McAndrews to verify that he was aware of Fenton's past."

"That's a good idea, Ferris. I'll do that. So that rules out the staff unless something new turns up. What about the members? Whose got a motive?"

"That's just it, sir. The only one that we can really tie in with Krieger is Mr. Kichler, if there's any truth to the rumors about his wife. But that was fifteen years ago. If there had been a real problem with their marriage, you would have thought they would have divorced or separated or something during that time, but they still seem to be happily married."

"Or at least married," McKernan interjected. "But again you make a good point. Unless there's something we don't know about, Kichler's motive would seem to be a pretty weak one."

"And none of the other members seem to have any sort of motive at all. At least that we know of."

"So where does that leave us, Ferris? We've seem to have come to the conclusion that no one had a motive, or at least one strong enough to lead to murder."

Ferris stared at his half-empty glass for a moment. "Maybe, we're looking at this the wrong way, sir."

"What do you mean?"

"Well, we've been looking at this from the possible suspects end of things. Maybe we should be looking more at the victim."

"In what way?"

"Well, what do we really know about the Krieger, anyway?"

"That's just it. We really don't know much about him at all. Not about his private life, not about his past."

"Exactly," Ferris said. "I really don't know much about this Rhodesian War thing. I was just a kid. Not even that, really. Do you think that it is a possibility that Krieger was really part of this 17 Commando?"

"There's no proof," McKernan answered. "Everything against him is circumstantial or hearsay. The only things we know for sure is that Krieger was involved in some sort of violent business back then, and that he's taken steps to alter his appearance. But there could be other reasons for that. We just can't ask him."

"But it is suspicious," Ferris persisted.

"Of course it's suspicious. But there could be reasonable explanations for the bullet wound and plastic surgery. Maybe he was a witness to some crime and he was in hiding from the criminals. Maybe he just didn't like his face. Plenty of people don't you know."

"Is there any way that we can check that? I mean about his being a witness in hiding."

"Probably not," McKernan said. "Even if he was part of some witness protection scheme, we wouldn't even know what agency to ask. Assuming that it was done officially."

"OK. Well, what if for the sake of argument we accept the fact that Krieger was part of this 17 Commando group? Where does that lead us?"

"Where *does* it lead us?"

"We've got two people who were present who lost someone they were close to as a result of 17 Commando, the chef and Mr. McAndrews."

"After twenty years?"

"In one case it was an older brother, in the other, the man who saved his life. Either one could be a pretty strong motive, sir. Certainly better than anything else we've come up against." It was clear Ferris was getting worked up about the idea.

"It still seems pretty thin to me, Ferris. It's been over twenty years. And we don't even have any real proof that Krieger was connected with 17 Commando or the Rhodesian War. When I talked to Otis he admitted that he couldn't be sure that it was him. And McAndrews isn't the kind of man who would act on something this important without being dead sure he was right."

"Pardon me for asking this, sir, but just how well *do* you know Mr. McAndrews?"

"I know him well enough to know he isn't a murderer, constable," Mckernan said emptying his glass and slamming it on the table.

"I'm sorry, sir," Ferris said after a moment. "I didn't mean—"

"No, Ferris. I'm the one who should apologize. I asked you to speak your mind. And you're right, I shouldn't let my personal feelings affect my judgment. Are you ready for another pint?"

"Another time, sir. I think I should get back to work. There might be some replies about missing cyanide."

"You're right, constable. We should both be getting back to work."

CHAPTER 24
MISSING CYANIDE

"Sir?" Constable Ferris said with an unusually serious look on his youthful face as he poked it into McKernan's office. The inspector had been taking a break from the case Tuesday morning to catch up on paperwork.

"What is it, Ferris?"

"I've had a message from one of the labs I contacted reporting that they are missing some potassium cyanide."

McKernan's ears pricked up, hoping this might be the break he'd been waiting for. "Which one?"

"It was Anglo-Martian's assay lab, sir," Ferris said gravely, acutely aware of the chief inspector's concern that the evidence pointing in the direction of his friend Otis McAndrews continued to pile up.

"I see. Who made the report?"

"Sheila Nelson, the chief chemist. Do you want me to follow up on it?"

McKernan thought for a moment before answering, "No, I think I'll do it myself. Have the other labs responded?"

"Most of them. None of them have reported missing any."

"OK. Get after the ones that you haven't heard from yet. I want to get this nailed down as soon as possible."

"Yes, sir."

Anglo-Martian had been one of the first of the corporations to move out of Hut Town when the first permanent portions of Mars City had been built. The corporate offices were now on the Concourse, but some of the technical operations were still in their original quarters, right off the corridor leading to the airlock for Hut Town's Corridor C. McKernan couldn't remember how many times he'd walked the length of that hallway in the six years he'd been on Mars.

A modest plaque attached to the fused silica brickwork marked the air-tight door that was the entrance to Anglo-Martian's Technical Services. The door was sealed, but not locked. The inspector stepped through into the small lobby where he was greeted by an earnest young man whose build indicated he was more security than receptionist.

"Chief Inspector McKernan. What can I do for you?" he asked deferentially.

"I'd like to speak to Ms. Nelson, if I may."

"She's been expecting you. Down the hall and the last door on the left. I'll let her know you're coming."

Some attempt had been made to enliven the bland plastic panels of the hallway walls with photographic prints of various Martian surface features. It wasn't completely successful, but McKernan approved of the fact that no attempt had been made to conceal the fact that they were buried beneath two meters of Martian soil and not on Earth.

Another discrete sign on the door announced "Assay Lab." McKernan knocked and entered without waiting for an invitation. The lab was a long, narrow room about fifteen by seven meters. A number of lab benches littered with glassware ran in a double row down the middle while various pieces of apparatus were arrayed along the back wall. The chief chemist was sitting at the bench nearest the door while several technicians worked in other parts of the laboratory.

"I've been expecting someone," Sheila Nelson said when she saw the inspector enter. The Chief Chemist was a trim woman in her late thirties with short-cropped brown hair just starting to show hints of gray. She'd been on Mars nearly five years and the tan of her face was the work of a UV lamp rather than the sun. The very picture of efficiency, she was dressed in a white lab coat over comfortable looking slacks. "I suppose that I'm in for it,"

"That depends. Why don't you tell me what happened," McKernan responded.

"It was last week. My normal procedure is to draw whatever reagents and supplies I expect to need during the week each Monday morning. There's usually a schedule of how many and what type of samples are to be tested, so I know what will be needed fairly precisely. The supplies are put in the appropriately labeled containers and put on that shelf," she said pointing to a shelf above one of the lab benches. Last Monday I drew 150 grams of potassium cyanide."

"That's quite a lot, isn't it?"

"It depends. If you're trying to poison people, you could probably kill several hundred, at least. If you're trying to extract certain minerals from several hundred kilograms of rock, it's pretty typical of what we use in a week."

"I see," McKernan said.

"Each time one of my staff needs some, they weigh it out on that balance over there." She pointed to a delicate apparatus housed inside a glass case. "The time and amount is recorded on the terminal next to it and charged to a project. Considering the cost of shipping supplies from Earth, the bean-counters like to keep tabs on things."

"On Thursday, I was going to weigh some out and I noticed that the amount in the bottle looked low. I weighed the contents, checked how much had been used, and noticed that 25 grams were missing."

"And you didn't notify anyone?" McKernan asked skeptically.

"At that time, nobody had died of cyanide poisoning," Nelson answered defensively. "The monetary value wasn't that great. I figured either one of my staff had forgotten to make an entry or some had been spilled or something. 25 grams is not a great deal, about the size of the tip of your little finger. I was concerned because it indicated someone had been sloppy not because they were homicidal."

"What did your staff say when you confronted them?"

"Confronted is a bit strong, inspector. I asked if anyone knew what had happened to the KCN."

"KCN?"

"That's the chemical formula for potassium cyanide inspector."

"And the answer was?"

"My staff, which consists of two whole technicians, both of whom are on their second contract, denied knowing anything about it. I tend to believe them."

"I don't suppose that an incorrect amount was withdrawn from the stockroom at the start of the week?"

"When your constable made his inquiry, I checked the amount in the stockroom, myself. The amount is within a gram of what it should be."

"Any chance the stockroom has been tampered with?"

"The room is always locked. Security and I have the only keys. That's it, there," she said, pointed to a room made of fused silica blocks with a very solid looking steel door.

"And access to this room?"

"It's locked up after hours. Not during the day. Of course there's usually someone working in here."

"At lunch time? Do you and your staff eat in here."

"It's not a good practice to eat around chemicals," Nelson responded disapprovingly. "There's a lunch room down the hall. If all three of us eat at the same time I lock the door, but we often take staggered breaks because we're in the middle of some procedure that can't be interrupted."

"Was anyone besides your staff in here that week?"

"Dozens of people. Sample deliveries, messengers, geologists impatient for results, the boss."

"The boss?"

"McAndrews. He was a pretty good field geologist in his day. He still likes to keep his hand in. Not so much the chemical end of thing, but for the geology. He's always taking slices of samples and looking at them through a microscope. He's a real hand's on guy." This she said approvingly.

"And you're sure he was in here around the time the cyanide went missing?"

Nelson looked at him in surprise. "You can't seriously suspect McAndrews, can you?"

"I'm a policeman. I was trained to suspect everyone."

"Well, I won't believe it."

"You don't have to, Ms. Nelson. But what about the others you mentioned. Anyone unusual amongst them."

"Not really. I know all the Anglo-Martian geologists, of course. Most of the messengers and deliverymen, too. I don't remember anyone I didn't recognize. Oh, there was that chubby guy from Transamerican. What's his name, Olberman. He had a rush sample in for analysis and he was in a hurry for the results. Don't know why. It was a complete bust. He was hanging around until it was finished."

"Is it usual for you to be doing analysis for other companies?"

"It's not unusual," Nelson answered, "at least not for some of the smaller outfits. McAndrews likes us to keep busy. We probably do a couple of outside jobs a week."

"Would it have been possible for any of these visitors to have accessed the potassium cyanide without being seen?"

Nelson looked thoughtful for a moment. "I suppose so, especially if one or more of us were out of the room. Our tests do require concentration, and if we're working under the hood—" she pointed to several fume hoods at the end of the room. "It can get noisy in here with the fans going."

"So, someone could have gotten the bottle down and knocked 25 grams into, say an envelope or something, without being seen?"

"Yes. It would have been possible. Damned dangerous thing to do, though."

"Murder is often dangerous, Ms. Nelson. Thank you for your time." With that the chief inspector turned leaving the chief chemist with an uncertain expression on her face.

By that afternoon, Ferris had been able to get responses from all of the labs that used cyanide. Not one of them had reported any missing. The several shops that used it in industrial quantities were less able to respond certainly, but none of them had any reason to suspect that they had any unexplained losses, either.

McKernan pondered these facts as he walked home along Corridor B in Hut Town. To say that he was troubled as to where the evidence was pointing would have been an understatement.

His concerns must have been visible on his face, for when Elisabeth looked up at him as he entered the hut she remarked, "You look tired, Erik. Is anything wrong? Is it the case?"

McKernan hesitated for a moment, then realized that there was no point in pretending that he wasn't bothered.

"Yeah, it's just dragging out more than I'd like."

"Aren't you getting anywhere?"

"I can't say that. The evidence is starting to add up. I'm just not very happy with where it's pointing."

"Oh? Why?"

"Bits and pieces keep implicating McAndrews. Nothing really solid, you understand. It's all circumstantial and I'm sure that any half-way competent defense lawyer back on Earth would have a field day refuting it with a jury, but I can't afford to ignore it, either."

"You don't really think that Otis is guilty, do you?"

"I really don't know. I know I don't want him to be guilty. But am I letting my feelings cloud my judgment? I'd feel a whole lot better if I knew with certainty that someone else was guilty."

"What are you going to do about it?" the doctor asked. She'd never known McKernan to be plagued by this much uncertainty, and it worried her.

"That's just it. I don't know. I can't ignore the evidence, but there's no smoking gun. Yet, if I put what I know in my report, Otis's reputation may be ruined even if he's eventually exonerated. I might destroy one of my best friends. Worse, there's no way to resolve things here on Mars. We don't have any courts, any juries. The fact is that we don't really even have any laws. All we have are Trust Authority bureaucrats. And I'm one of them."

"Do you have to do anything?" Beth asked. "I mean if you aren't certain of who did it. Can't you just put in your report, 'party or parties unknown' or something like that?"

"Somebody killed Krieger. It's my job to find out who. Even if it is

Otis McAndrews. There's nothing else I can do."

"I know, Erik," the doctor said, knowing there was nothing she could do to help.

CHAPTER 25
LOOSE ENDS

"Mr. Kichler, could I have a moment of your time?" McKernan asked, having run into the gentleman as the inspector was heading to the room they had been using for their interviews. It was Wednesday morning and McKernan was back at the Mars Club because Kichler had finally returned from his field trip. Their meeting was not an accident.

"Of course, inspector, but I already gave my statement the night of the murder. I doubt that there is much I can add." Kichler was a handsome man in his mid forties, his features a blend of the Latin and teutonic.

"If you could come this way, I won't take up more than a minute or two of your time," the inspector said steering him to the back room. "You've been a difficult man to track down, Mr. Kichler."

"I've been busy. We had some issues at one of our installations."

"I understand, sir. Please, have a seat."

"What would you like to know, inspector?"

"The first thing is do you have anything to add to your statement about your movements that night?"

"No, I think that it should be accurate."

"I'm just checking, you understand. Things were a bit rushed that night."

"Of course."

"Just how well did you know Mr. Krieger?" McKernan asked in an off-hand manner.

"Not well. He was a very reserved man."

"So I'm finding," the inspector agreed. "It's just that it seems that he'd spent quite a bit of time in Rio and Montevideo ten or fifteen years ago. That's where you're from, isn't it? I thought you might have crossed paths with him back then, being in the same line of work."

Kichler seemed to tense. "Yes, I was introduced to him on several occasions, but we were never more than the most casual of acquaintances."

"Some of the social columns of the time portray him as a rather dashing character. Quite a change from how people here have been describing him, isn't it?"

"Yes. He could be very charming when it suited him, but mostly that was with the ladies," Kichler remarked with disapproval.

McKernan looked across the table at the other man. "Was your wife one of those that found him charming?"

"I see you've dug up some of the old dirt, inspector. You must understand that there was never any truth to the rumors. Rio Plata was just starting then. I was often in the field. Krieger escorted my wife to a concert or two, the ballet. But nothing more. My wife and I are happily married with two children. What may or may not have happened is in the past. Do you understand? And, no, to answer your question, I did not kill Krieger over something that didn't happen over a decade ago."

"Do you have any idea who did?"

"No. I'm afraid that I can't help you inspector. Will there be anything else?"

"No, that will be all for the moment. Thank you," McKernan answered. After Kichler had left, he pondered as to what he had learned. Kichler had certainly reacted when he had mentioned the rumors about his wife, but were they the reactions of a murderer?

Constable Ferris was walking down the corridor of the Mars Club. He was looking for Chief Inspector McKernan because he had received a reply from one of the inquiries he had been instructed to send to Earth. What he found, however, was Mrs. Simpson who was busily vacuuming the already immaculate carpet.

"Mrs. Simpson, you haven't seen the inspector, have you?"

"I believe that Mr. McKernan is in the room in the back, constable. I was just tidying up the back hall before this and I saw him through the door."

"Thank you, Mrs. Simpson," Ferris said politely. He'd been at the job long enough to know when a kind word would work better than the third degree. "It's a shame about your husband. You have my condolences."

"Why, thank you, constable," Mrs. Simpson responded a bit puzzled. "Alf was a good sort, really. I do miss him."

"Did they ever catch the driver of the car?"

"No, they never did, more's the pity. Folks like that shouldn't be allowed to drive. The policeman working the case said they had what he called a lead at one point. Part of the number plate it was. But I guess that never amounted to anything."

"Did the police ever go into the details with you?"

"No, they never did, constable. And, to tell the truth, I never asked them. I was too broken up about Alf and trying to deal with the hotel all at the same time. It just didn't seem important."

"No, I guess it wouldn't. Still, it's too bad the driver was never charged. Well, thank you again, Mrs. Simpson. Have a nice day," Ferris said as he headed towards the interview room.

"You're welcome, constable," Mrs. Simpson replied, a bit befuddled by the whole exchange.

"What is it, Ferris?" McKernan asked, looking up when Ferris entered the room. "You look like a cat with a canary."

"We got the reply back from the British authorities about the accident investigation on Mrs. Simpson's husband. They sent a copy of the case file and the investigator's notes."

"Anything interesting?"

"According to the report he was run over by a black BMW. There was a witness, but they only got a portion of the license number, the last three digits. The police were never able to match that with a car, though. Coincidentally, the numbers did match those of the license for a BMW owned by a Peter Krieger. He was interviewed, but was able to provide a rock solid alibi, literally. He had been at some geology symposium in London at the time. Plenty of witnesses. The police looked at his car, but as Krieger had gone to France after the symposium it wasn't until several weeks after the accident. Oddly enough, the car had recently been repainted silver. There was no way for the police to prove anything and Krieger was represented by a very high powered firm of solicitors. That line of investigation was dropped and no charges were ever filed."

"You seem to have something more to say on the subject, constable."

"Yes, sir. I ran into Mrs. Simpson vacuuming in the hallway. I asked her about her husband's death. She said that she had never heard any of the details of the investigation, so she isn't aware of any link to Krieger."

"And you believe her?"

"Yes, sir. The information about Krieger was never released to the press by the police."

"She might have found out later. After all, you did."

"I don't think so, sir. Mrs. Simpson doesn't strike me as a good liar."

McKernan smiled. "I think you'll find there's more to Mrs. Simpson than what's on the surface."

"Still, if she doesn't know about the connection that leaves her without a motive."

"That we know of. But your point is taken, constable. In any case, it was good police work on your part. And now, I think it might be time to have a word with the chef about his brother. Why don't you go down to the kitchen and see if you can round him up."

It was less than two minutes before Ferris returned with chef Duro. Ferris motioned him towards a chair and then took a seat at the table.

"Thank you for coming, chef," McKernan began cordially. "There are just a few points I'd like to clear up."

"Will this take long, inspector? I'm right I the middle of getting ready for lunch. You understand the members can be difficult if it's late."

"This should only take a few minutes. I've just a few questions."

The chef seemed relieved. "Of course, anyway I can be of help."

"Good. Now after the dinner you were in the kitchen while your assistant was in the dining room cleaning tables. Is that correct?" McKernan made a point of not starting out with what he was interested in.

"Yes. I told you that before."

"You said you saw Teague come down for some bottles. We're trying to establish how long he was gone from the bar."Did you happen to see when he went back up?"

"No, but as I said, from where I was in the kitchen I couldn't see the stairs. But I think I did hear when he closed the storeroom door. I was waiting for the next cart to come down in the elevator, so it was quiet in the kitchen. I'm not sure how much later it was, though. Maybe ten minutes, a little less. Sorry I can't be more precise."

"Oh, that's alright. At least it helps us establish that he was down in the storeroom for some time, which is important. And you didn't see or hear anyone else going up and down the stairs during that time."

"No, but during that time I was loading things into the dishwasher. Banging the pots and such."

"Yes, of course. Quite understandable. Thank you. I think that about does it. Oh, there is one more thing. Your file mentions that you have a brother who is also a chef. Is that where you learned your craft?"

"Sadly, no," the chef answered with a sigh. "My brother died while I was still a young boy. I never got the chance to work with him. But I remember hearing his stories about all the places he had worked. That was what inspired me to become a chef. It seemed so glamorous."

"I'm sorry to hear about your brother. If you don't mind my asking, how did he die?"

Duro looked up in surprise. "No. I don't mind. It was a long time ago. He was working as a sous chef at a resort in Angola, the sort of place for wealthy tourists to safari with first class food and wine. There was a sort of bush dinner, tents and white coated waiters. I never got all the details, but they were in the wrong place at the wrong time. Some rebels had crossed over the border from Zimbabwe. They started shooting without knowing it was just a group of tourists. My brother and several others were killed. It was all so senseless. I'm not even sure if they had a gun in the camp."

"Did they find the men responsible?"

"I don't think so. We never heard much back in Portugal. And, as I said, I was still a kid. I knew nothing about rebels and civil wars at the time."

"Well, we've taken up enough of your time, chef. Thank you, again. You've been very helpful."

After Duro had left McKernan asked Ferris, "Well, do you think our chef is telling the truth?"

"About not having any idea that there might be a link between Krieger and his brother's death? Yeah, it sounds to me like he was just a kid whose brother died in some far off place. It didn't seem like he knew any of the details. What do you think, sir?"

"Me? I'd be willing to bet you're right. And, after all, we don't even know for sure that Krieger ever was a part of 17 Commando. I think we can put the chef towards the bottom of our list of suspects."

"So where does that leave us, sir?"

"I'm not sure, Ferris. I'm not sure. We've got four subjects for whom revenge might be a motive, five if you count Duckworth."

"Duckworth, sir?" Ferris interrupted. "I don't understand."

"I don't know if you've noticed, constable, but Mr. Duckworth seems to have intentions towards Mrs. Simpson. He might have wanted to kill Krieger to get in good with the housekeeper. Or they might have conspired together to kill the man responsible for her husband's death."

"But Mrs. Simpson doesn't seem to have had any idea that it was Krieger's car that killed her husband."

"No, that's just it. She doesn't know, if we believe her, and if she doesn't, then we can rule her out, and Duckworth as well. Just as the chef doesn't seem to know much about his brother's death, either."

"And Mr. Kichler?" Ferris asked, having guessed the other possible suspects.

"Mr. Kichler claims the incident is water under the bridge. Unfortunately for us, I have no reason not to believe him."

"But, sir. That leaves only—"

"Yes, constable. That only leaves Mr. McAndrews with a possible motive."

"But surely you don't think that he's the murderer?" Ferris asked. The constable was only too well aware of the relationship between McAndrews and the inspector.

"I certainly don't want to, constable," McAndrews replied.

CHAPTER 26
FINNEGAN'S AGAIN

McKernan had received a text message from Elisabeth saying that something had come up and she would be pulling a double shift at the hospital. He didn't feel like going home to an empty hut at that moment. Instead, he turned into Finnegan's.

McKernan took a seat at the bar. The place was empty except for a couple sitting at a table in the back and a man McKernan recognized as the head of the power systems department who was sitting at the bar nursing a beer.

"You look as if you could use a drink, inspector," Finnegan asked. He was the only one tending bar, which wasn't surprising. He always tended bar, usually alone, except when things got busy Friday nights and Sunday afternoons. "The usual?" That was the great thing about Finnegan's. It was the kind of place where most of the patrons were regulars, and most of them had a "usual" which the bartender always remembered.

"Sure," McKernan assented. "you might be seeing more of me in the future." He wasn't sure why he had added that. There had been a time, before he had met the doctor, when he had been a regular.

Finnegan cocked a white eye-brow. "Trouble at home, inspector?"

"Elisabeth's contract is coming up. She's applied for a position on Earth. There's a good chance she'll take it."

"That's too bad, inspector. I liked that one. Mars needs women like that."

"Tell her that," Mckernan said.

Finnegan picked up a spotless glass from the back bar, wiped it with the towel that was always in his hand, and set it on the bar in front of McKernan. Turning back to the bar he brought down a bottle from the top shelf and poured three fingers of the amber liquid into the glass. After a moment's consideration he fetched a second glass a poured another measure.

"To your health, inspector," Finnegan toasted as he raised his glass to his lips.

"Slange," McKernan responded.

"So, have you told her that you want her to stay?" Finnegan asked idly polishing a wine glass.

"How can I? She hates Mars. She hates living in a tin can. She's said so. She hates not being able to go outside without a surface suit. She *wants* to go back to Earth."

"Maybe she does," Finnegan conceded, "but have you given her a reason to stay?"

McKernan looked at the bar owner.

"It could be, inspector, that what she wants most is a sense of permanence, of belonging. Have you offered her that?"

"In my line of work? On Mars?"

"You've survived this long, Erik. There's no reason to think you won't live to a ripe old age."

"Or die of a cracked face-plate or failed life-support pack or a knife to the belly trying to break up a bar fight."

"And if you were a copper back on Earth you could end up just as dead from a dozen different causes. That's the nature of existence, boyo."

McKernan sank into silence studying the surface of the whisky in his glass.

Finnegan, with the age-old instinct of a bartender, changed the subject. "So how goes it with the 'Case of the Poisoned Port?'"

McKernan laughed. "Is everyone calling it that?"

"Why not? It's accurate, isn't it. And you have to admit, it's the most interesting thing to have happened on Mars in a long time. Our very own mystery among our very own gentry. Poison in the palace. Cyanide in the castle. Ah, if only we had our own newspaper. There'd be some grand headlines to titillate the populace."

"How did the word get out?"

"You surprise me, inspector. Mars City is just a small town, and small towns have no secrets. Dr. Greenwood was in and dropped a few hints over his cocktail. Your own Sergeant Gaeretts tried to squash a few rumors. Everybody on the concourse has been marking the comings and goings of you and Constable Ferris from the Mars Club at all hours of the day and night. Come, man, how could you keep a thing like that under wraps."

"I suppose it was hopeless from the start," McKernan said with a shrug.

"So, have you figured out who done it?"

"Not yet, too many suspects, not enough evidence."

"Cheer up, inspector. I've every confidence in you. You'll work it out before long."

"Sure," McKernan responded, draining his glass and debating whether to have another. "Tell me, bar keep. Do any of the members of the Mars Club ever drop in here?"

"Care for another?" Finnegan asked. McKernan nodded. As he was pouring the drink he said, "Well, Otis comes in fairly regularly. But then we've known each other a long time. As to the others, not so often."

"I didn't think they would, with the club just across the way."

"Oh, Kenji will drop by from time to time on Sundays to watch the football match. And that American chap, what's his name, Olberman.   He comes in for a martini late afternoons when it's quiet."

"Oh?" McKernan said, suddenly interested.

"Yes. Makes a fairly regular habit of it. Though if you ask me, and mind you this is a bartender speaking, he probably shouldn't. That man drinks way too much and for all the wrong reasons."

"I've noticed," McKernan agreed.   "Ever talk to him much?"

"Inspector!   I'm shocked.   Isn't the conversation between   a   bartender   and   a   drunk   privileged communication?"

"Not in any jurisdiction I've ever heard of."

"Well it should be. Come home rule for Mars I'll make sure it's written into the constitution."

"You do that, Finnegan.   But for now, what did Olberman say?"

"It's not so much any one thing. Just little bits here and there.   I gather business has not been so good and the powers that be back on Earth have been wondering what he's been doing up here on Mars."

"Any details?"

"Well, it's no secret that Transamerican has had a couple of concessions that haven't panned out. They could use a big hit. Olberman has been working on one, but there's been competition, mostly from Pretoria."

McKernan remembered the article Ferris's friend had found. "I've heard something along those lines, myself."

"I gather, also, that Mr. Olberman, or more accurately, the ex-Mrs. Olberman has been living above her budget."

"Ex-Mrs. Olberman?   I wasn't aware that they were divorced," McKernan said, suddenly attentive.

"Well, I gather it's not official yet," Finnegan clarified. "But his wife has said she intends to separate, though how you can be more separate than living on different planets is beyond me. In any case, more than once Olberman has been in here lamenting the fact that his wife spent too much of his money and has never appreciated the sacrifices he'd made for his family. From what he said, it's the fact that he hasn't been back on Earth in three years that's strained his marriage. It's a shame, too, because he really does seem to love his daughters."

"It's surprising that he's lasted this long on Mars with family troubles like that," McKernan commented.

"I think that one of the reason's Olberman ended up on Mars, was the hardship pay his company gives out, not to mention the promise of a promotion on his return. But he won't get that if he doesn't make a success of things here. Lately he's seemed worried about whether he'd have enough money to support his wife and daughters in the style they've been accustomed to."

"Worried enough to consider doing something desperate?" McKernan queried.

Finnegan raised an eyebrow. "Oh, Mr. Olberman has his worries, right enough. But murder? He never seemed the type."

"No, I guess not," McKernan agreed. Though what type was it that poisoned a man's port?

"He always seemed harmless enough. Family man. Kept showing me pictures of his kids, two daughters. Just about old enough to be thinking about going to university."

"And college is expensive in America. Especially the good schools," McKernan observed.

"Still, it would be a quite a stretch to believe he'd commit murder."

"Did he ever mention Krieger?"

"Only to say that he'd been trying to work out some sort of deal on the concession. Some sort of arrangement where the two companies would operate it jointly."

"Was Krieger agreeable?"

"Olberman didn't say. He did call Krieger a tough old Afrikaaner bastard once. But he'd been drinking pretty heavily at the time. I had to cut him off and send him home. Fortunately, that's just the other side of the Concourse."

"Yes. At least drunk driving isn't something we have to worry about on Mars."

"Thank goodness, for small favors," Finnegan said, excusing himself to tend to the couple at one of the tables for a moment.

It was something to think about, though, McKernan considered. From what he'd seen, Olberman was drinking much of the time, not necessarily drunk, but under the influence. Could that have decreased his inhibitions? Enough to commit murder? He'd seen plenty of drunks go after each other with knives in a bar fight then make up when they'd sobered up after a night in the drunk tank. But what about a cold blooded act like a poisoning? Could a man be so uninhibited from drinking as to deliberately poison someone? There was no doubt that Olberman had been drinking at dinner that night. But to poison Krieger, he would have had to have had the cyanide on him, and that would have involved premeditation. Unlikely, but something to think about.

Finnegan returned from his other customers. "Another, inspector?

"Not tonight, thank you. I think it's time for me to go home."

The lights were off when he entered the hut. It seemed colder than usual, as if Beth's absence had sucked the warmth out. Outside he could hear the wind blowing the dust against the thin skin of the hut. It had been over a year since the doctor had moved in with him, since it had become not just a hut but a home. He'd been alone before that. Soon he might well be alone again, the hut empty except for himself.

He considered having another drink from the special bottle that he kept. In the end he decided against it. Now was a time to keep his wits about him. Instead, he went to bed and waited for Beth.

CHAPTER 27
SCOTCH REVELATIONS

"How is the investigation going?" McAndrews asked as he caught McKernan in the corridor outside the lounge of the Mars Club. It was Thursday evening, and McKernan had been reviewing the notes of the case hoping to achieve some sort of clarity. He'd found that the quiet of the room they'd been using for interviews offered fewer distractions than his office at the station. He also realized, that progress or not, he'd soon have to give it up.

"About the same, sir. Too many suspects and too few clues," the inspector responded pensively.

"You seem troubled by that, Erik. Perhaps it would help if you discussed the case with someone. I'm free at the moment. Why don't we have a seat in the lounge and we can talk it over?"

McKernan was on the point of refusing, then seemed to come to a sudden decision.

"Perhaps you are right at that, sir. It might help me to clear the air a bit."

McAndrews led them into the lounge and to a pair of seats off to the side. At that hour the lounge was empty except for Stan Olberman who was sitting at a table in a far corner writing. It seemed unlikely that he would be able to overhear their conversation.

"So what exactly is troubling you, Erik? It's clear that something is on your mind."

The inspector sat in silence for a moment, weighing heavily exactly what he was going to say. Then he began,

"From the start it was obvious that nearly everyone who was in the club that night had the opportunity to tamper with the glass of port while it sat on the bar. Too many people had a period of a minute or so when they could have slipped into the bar without being observed."

"I assume you are including me in that list?" McAndrews commented.

"Yes, I am," the inspector replied sharply. "Kenji Fujika saw you leaving the restroom as he was going in. Presumably you passed through the bar both before and afterwards. This was in the period after Teague had placed the port on the bar and gone down to the storeroom in the cellar."

"But surely others had the same opportunity?" McAndrews objects.

"Of course, sir. Kenji for one. Stan Olberman was another. He entered the restroom just as Kenji was leaving. From their statements we know several other members used the lavatory as well during the period in question, not to mention those that just passed through the bar on their way to the lounge or billiard room. That doesn't even include the staff, all of whom had at least an opportunity to go into the bar area unobserved. So you see my problem, at least as far as having an opportunity to poison the port. At least half a dozen people had a clear shot at it and it can't be ruled out as a possibility for most of the rest of the people who were in the club that night. Unfortunately, though, there's no physical evidence linking any one person to the crime."

"I can see your problem, Erik," McAndrews said sympathetically. "But surely you have other approaches to identifying the suspect?"

"Yes. The obvious thing is to look for a motive. Sane, rational people don't just go about poisoning other people without a strong reason. And the one thing about Mars is that nearly everyone has to go through rigorous psychological screening before they're allowed to come here. So I've looked for a motive. The problem with that is that Krieger has been a particularly secretive individual. Either that, or he really did not have much of a past, which I find hard to believe for a person in his position."

The club secretary looked off into an unseen distance. "You're right about Krieger being secretive, Erik. He's been coming to Mars off and on for the last six years. I've had business dealings with the man and his company, I've attended numerous social functions, he's been a member of the club almost from its founding, yet in all that time I can't remember him revealing anything about his personal life. But his being a reserved or a particularly private individual isn't really a motive I wouldn't have thought."

"No, it isn't. And what few details I've been able to uncover that might provide a motive are little more than rumors or coincidence. For example, did you know that the car that killed Mrs. Simpson's husband had the same last three digits as one that was registered to Peter Krieger? Of course, he claimed that he wasn't even in the country at the time and provided witnesses to that affect. And I'm don't believe that Mrs. Simpson is even aware of this fact. I discovered it from the police report of the incident. There was gossip, too of an affair between Krieger and Leo Kichler's wife a dozen years ago, but it may just have been gossip. Kichler is still married, happily so, he claims."

"Neither of those would seem to be promising as a motive," McAndrews commented.

"No, but it did cause me to delve into Krieger's past. The problem is, is that before fifteen years ago it doesn't exist. No employment history, no university degree, no school records, not one scrap of public information about the man. All of which lends credence to the governor's allegation that Krieger had something to hide, perhaps his belonging to 17 Commando. And that would certainly provide motivation for at least a few people."

"In what way?" McAndrews asked cautiously.

"17 Commando's reign of terror might have been short, but it turns out it affected more than a few people who were present that night. For example, the chef's brother was killed during a cross border raid into Angola where he had been working at a resort. And the governor might have been motivated for political or philosophical reasons."

"Again, I assume you are including me in that number?" McAndrews asked.

"You can't deny that your experiences while a prisoner of 17 Commando might well provide a motive?"

"No, of course not. But I've never been sure that Krieger and the man I knew as the leader of 17 Commando were one and the same. It was a long time ago, Erik. I can't be sure of what I remember. Not to the point of swearing to it in a court of law."

"But you certainly had your suspicions, sir. If so, why have you never brought them to the attention of any one. To the Trust Authority, for example."

"Because I never had any proof. You don't accuse a man of being a mass murderer and a terrorist without some sort of tangible proof. At least I don't. Not least of all because of the possibility of a suit of slander. Mars doesn't need that kind of publicity right now. You know that, Erik."

The inspector wasn't sure how to respond to that. He looked down at the carpet at his feet. When he looked up again it was to see Jeeves who had managed to approach noiselessly.

"Is there anything I can bring you, sir?" the butler asked.

"Will you join me in a Scotch, Erik?" McAndrews asked.

"Thank you, sir. I think I could use one."

"Two Scotch's, with just a splash. From my private bottle."

"Of course, Mr. McAndrews."

After the butler was gone, McAndrews jested, "Are you sure Jeeves didn't do it?"

"He or Teague certainly had the best chance to poison the port without anyone noticing," the inspector replied seriously. "But I haven't been able to find any sort of motive for either one. Unless one of them is a paid assassin."

"I hope you're joking, Erik," McAndrews responded.

"Just how cut-throat is the competition between mining companies?" Erik asked a moment later. He had been distracted by Olberman leaving the room.

"I would certainly hope it hasn't stooped to that level," McAndrews answered. "But, go on. You seem to have eliminated some of your suspects through lack of motive. Doesn't that help?"

"In a way, yes. It does narrow the field. Which leaves us with means, that last of the three classic factors in detection. Who had access to cyanide? You were right when you said that it was used in mining and metallurgy. We've checked into that, and it is used in fairly large quantities by several operations. Fortunately, they tend to keep a fairly close eye on it. Also, most of it isn't in a form suitable for poisoning port. Nor was I able to find a time when any of the likely suspects would have had access to those sources."

"Of course, potassium cyanide also has uses in analysis, and most of the chemical laboratories have some in their stockrooms, usually in crystalline or powdered form. Ideal for slipping into a drink. Surprisingly, they seem less careful with their supplies than the industrial users. Several of the labs we contacted couldn't be sure that a small quantity wasn't missing. I'm sorry to say Anglo-Martian's assay lab was one of them. And it would only have taken a few grams to have killed Krieger."

"That's a serious allegation, Erik. It almost sounds as if you think I might have been the murderer."

"I certainly would like to believe you weren't sir, but you see my dilemma. It would appear that you had the opportunity, a motive, and access to the means. Of course, I have no proof—"

"Your drinks, gentlemen," Jeeves interrupted, placing a tray with the two Scotches on the table between their chairs.

McAndrews stared at the inspector, trying desperately to decide how to respond. He was about to say something when Ferris appeared in the doorway.

"If you'll excuse me for a moment, sir," the inspector said as he got up to consult with the constable.

When he returned to his chair he found McAndrews sitting silently, the glass of Scotch held in his hand. Taking his seat he reached for his own glass. He was about to take a sip when McAndrews said coldly, "Erik, if you value your life, I advise you not to take a sip from that glass."

"Why—?"

"Smell it, lad."

Cautiously he held his nose over the glass. Not quite masked by the peat and alcohol of the Scotch was something else, the same aroma he had sensed in the poisoned glass of port.

"I believe that if you have the contents of your glass analyzed you will find the presence of potassium cyanide."

"But how could you detect the odor of my drink from your seat, sir?"

"I couldn't, Erik. I detected it in mine."

He passed over his glass to the inspector who detected the same scent of bitter almonds as he had in his own glass. Setting the glass down on the tray he noticed the corner of a folded piece of a paper sticking out from under the paper napkin.

Unfolding it he found a short note penned in neat block letters and signed "Otis McAndrews." It was a suicide note confessing to the murder of Peter Krieger and Chief Inspector McKernan. Silently he handed the note over the McAndrews.

"You can't believe I wrote this, Erik? Can you?"

"No, sir. If you will excuse me for a moment."

The inspector stood up and left the lounge. When he returned a few minutes later he resumed his seat.

"You have to believe that I didn't murder Krieger, nor did I intend to poison you, Erik."

"Oh, I believe you, sir. I know you didn't kill Krieger, but now I know who did." He found himself reaching for his Scotch, but then thought better of it.

"I take it you aren't going to tell me?"

"Not at this time, sir. But you will find out soon enough."

"It's a pity," McAndrews said, shaking his head, "it was a very good Scotch."

CHAPTER 28
I'VE GATHERED YOU TOGETHER

McKernan waited until the last of the members had gone up to the Cupola before he made his entrance. He ascended the narrow stairs to the landing and then stepped through the airlock into the circular room. There was a fair amount of dust in the atmosphere, and as it was a few minutes before sunset, the sky shown with a reddish glow that faded into nearly black at the zenith.

They were all there, all the members of the Mars Club that had been present for the dinner, Otis McAndrews, Kenji Fujika, Stan Olberman, Wu Lin, Francois DuChene, Leo Kichler, Robert Gordon, Helmut Nordlund, and Boris Kasperovski. The Trust Authority Governor, Louis Tsangambo was there as well, sitting, unbeknownst to himself, in the very chair that Peter Krieger had died in. The staff of the Mars Club were in attendance as well, Fenton, Teague, Duckworth, Mrs. Simpson, and of course William Watson, better known as Jeeves. Jose Duro and Alphonso Allicante were there in their chef's whites looking somewhat out of place. Constable Ferris stood off to one side while Sergeant Gaeretts had unobtrusively taken up a position in close proximity to the airlock which served as the only means of egress from the room.

Drinks had been laid on and a few of the members sat with cocktails in their hands. Somewhat self-consciously Mrs. Simpson held a small glass of sherry, while Walter Duckworth stood somewhat protectively just behind her, a rather larger glass of Scotch in his hand.

As the inspector emerged from the lock he glanced around the room, noting with interest the expressions on the various faces. Most looked a bit puzzled, one or two were amused. A few looked worried.

"Gentlemen," McKernan began, "and lady," he corrected, nodding in the direction of Mrs. Simpson who looked down at her sherry in embarrassment at the attention. "You are probably wondering why I have asked you all up here this evening."

"It does seem a bit melodramatic, Inspector," the governor commented acerbicly. "Can we assume that it *does* have something to do with the death of the late Mr. Krieger?"

"The governor, of course, is correct," the inspector replied. "I intend to reveal the name of the person responsible for the murder of Peter Krieger, who as you all know was murdered while sitting in this room exactly one week ago. Poisoned, in fact, while sitting in the very chair currently occupied by the governor."

If this revelation made any impression on Tsangambo he did an excellent job of hiding it. "I'm sure that we are all interested in hearing what you have to say, Inspector, but was it necessary for us all to be brought together in what might pass for a drawing room as if this were the final chapter of some British detective yarn from the twentieth century?"

"I do have my reasons, governor, which I will try to explain," McKernan replied. "I also will present the results of my investigation and the chain of evidence that has led me to my conclusions as to who committed the crime and how it was done."

"You make it sound as if this were a court of law and we were a jury," the governor protested.

"In a way you are," McKernan responded, his tone suddenly more serious. "It is one of the quirks of our position here on Mars that there is in fact no criminal justice system in place. Mars is currently administered as a trust territory under the administration of the United Nations Trust Authority. However, the agreements under which the Trust Authority was established make no provision for a legal code or for the judicial apparatus to administer such a code. The Trust Authority can, at its discretion, remove any person determined to have behaved in a manner detrimental to public safety or order such a person back to Earth, but that is a determination based on the private judgment of the governor, with input from the head of the public security agency, that is myself. However, there is no process with which to decide the guilt or innocence of an accused, no forum for the accused to defend himself, and in fact, no actual laws that one could be found guilty of violating.

"For typical situations such as miners getting drunk and fighting, this hasn't been an issue. Anyone who has caused too much trouble has been shipped back to Earth. The rest are allowed to sleep it off and go back to work. In the few cases of serious crime which have occurred, the guilt of the culprit has been obvious. Either that, or the problem has been resolved because the offender has died. At least a few of those by my own hand.

"But, with the murder of Peter Krieger, we find ourselves with a novel situation facing us. An act has occurred which in any jurisdiction on Earth would be a most serious offense, and anyone found guilty of it would be punished most severely. Yet, here on Mars, there is in fact no law against murder and no court capable of determining the guilt or innocence of one who stands accused of such a crime."

"That's preposterous," someone said.   It was Robert Gordon.

"I'm afraid the Chief Inspector has summed up the situation quite accurately," Otis McAndrews said calmly. "That is one of the issues that the committee arguing for home rule has been bringing up for the past few years."

"And as Mr. McAndrews must realize, that is a matter that must be decided on Earth by the United Nations," the governor broke in. "But, at least for the present, what the Chief Inspector has stated is true. There are no courts of law on Mars. My question, Inspector, is what exactly are you suggesting?"

"Under the Trust Authority charter, the only sanction that can be enforced is the removal of a criminal to Earth. Presumably, once there, the accused would fall under the jurisdiction of his home country and could be tried under those laws. But that is a problem to be sorted out back on Earth.   What I am proposing is that I will present the evidence and if it is found convincing the accused will be taken into custody and returned to Earth to be dealt with there."

"And you are suggesting that the people in this room act as judge and jury?" the governor asked.

"As the decision is ultimately yours, governor, you are the de facto judge and I would be presenting my report to you. As to the people gathered in this room, the members of the Mars Club are the most powerful men on the planet representing those entities most interested in the outcome, and as the murderer is, without a doubt, present in this room, I think that we can consider that this assemblage could be considered a 'jury of his peers,' at least in the sense it is construed in those parts of Earth where the criminal system is based on English common law."

"An interesting proposition, Inspector," the governor said. "And as you acknowledge, the final decision rests with me. Very well. I see no reason why we shouldn't proceed with your little drama. Carry on. But try not to make it too long. Who do you think is the murderer, inspector?"

"Jeeves the butler did it." McKernan said calmly.

CHAPTER 29
OPPORTUNITY

For a moment the group held their breath. Jeeves stood very still, a tray of drinks held in his hand, with a look of alarm on his face.

"Is this some kind of joke, Inspector?" the governor asked pointedly.

"Perhaps," the inspector replied. "There is no doubt that one week ago William Watson, better known as Jeeves, delivered a glass of port laced with cyanide to Peter Krieger in this very room, the glass of port that resulted in his death. We've made a thorough search of Krieger's body and effects as well as his suite of rooms on the floor below without finding the slightest trace of any poison. Also, the investigation has uncovered nothing that would lead one to conclude that the victim was of a state of mind to kill himself. Quite the contrary, everything about Mr. Krieger's personality would make that possibility seem highly unlikely. I feel confident that suicide can be ruled out.

"Jeeves was the last one to handle the fatal glass of port. His act of serving it resulted in Krieger's death. The question then becomes, 'Did Jeeves place the cyanide in the port, or was he aware that the port had been poisoned?' I will leave that question open for the time being."

"That's hardly fair, Erik, is it?" McAndrews objected.

"Perhaps not," McKernan answered. "From the beginning, this case has presented the problem of there being too many suspects. Jeeves has certainly been one of them. But *not* the only one." There was a rustling as those seated shifted uneasily.

"It's almost a cliché of detective fiction to say that there are three elements to solving a crime; opportunity, motive, and means. Let's then examine the facts of this case in those terms.

"First, let us address opportunity. The dinner broke up at approximately 2100. Before leaving the dining room, Peter Krieger placed his order for a glass of port to be served up in this room. This was not unusual behavior on his part, as he did it most nights and I think it safe to say that most if not all the members of the club who were at the dinner were aware of this habit. Certainly all the staff would have been.

"At 2110, give or take a few minutes, Jeeves made his request for the port to Teague who was manning the bar. Jeeves then left to take after dinner drink orders from the other diners who were in the process of dispersing to the lounge, the billiard room or the library. Teague, poured the glass of port and left it standing on a tray on the bar for Jeeves to pick up upon his return. Realizing that he was low on several types of spirits that he was likely to need during the evening, Teague left the bar to go down to the stockroom on the lower level. He was gone some ten minutes. Meanwhile, Jeeves, having collected the drink orders, returned to the bar, and finding Teague absent, picked up the tray with the glass of port, walked up the two flights of stairs to the Cupola and served the port to Krieger, who was sitting in a chair preparing to smoke his nightly cigar.

"I'm sorry to take so long dwelling on this, gentlemen, but those ten or so minutes between the time Teague poured the port and the time Jeeves served it are absolutely critical to the case, because it is during that interval that the cyanide was introduced into the glass.

"Logic will tell us that there are three and only three possibilities. One is that Teague poisoned the port immediately after pouring it and before he went to the stockroom. The second is that Jeeves added the cyanide somewhere during his trip to the Cupola. The third possibility is that some *other* person dropped the cyanide into the port as it was sitting on the bar after Teague had departed for the stockroom and before Jeeves had picked up the tray."

"Some other person, inspector? Who do you have in mind?" Kenji Fujika asked.

"That's just the problem, Kenji. As far as I have been able to establish from my interviews, each and every one of the people in this room had at least the possibility of entering the bar area unobserved and dropping the cyanide into the glass of port. The act, itself, would have only taken a matter of a few seconds."

"Everyone in the room, Chief Inspector? Certainly you are exaggerating," Fenton said.

"No, I don't think so," McKernan responded. "And to prove it, I will enumerate the possibilities. Note, I say the possibilities, because obviously only one person poisoned the port.

"Teague and Jeeves I've already covered. As to the rest of the staff, the assistant chef Alphonso Allicante was clearing up the dishes in the dining room. From there it is only a short step to the bar. After the last of the diners had left the room he could easily have done so without anyone noticing him.

"Chef Duro was alone in the kitchen on the lower level. He could easily have come up the stairs unobserved. The stairs open up to the corridor right next to the bar. As to

Mrs. Simpson and William Duckworth, the janitor, they were both watching videos in different rooms of the lower level. Either one of them could have made it to the stairway without being seen by the other or by Chef Duro, who was, if he is innocent, busily cleaning up in the kitchen out of view of the foot of the stairway."

"You seem to have left off one person, Erik," McAndrews noted.

"Quite correct. I have so far omitted the club steward, Fenton. After the dinner ended, he came into the dining room, had a few words with the governor and some of the members, and then returned to his office, which is conveniently located just the other side of the wall from the bar. He could easily have waited in the hall until he was sure of not being seen and made a quick visit to the bar or passed through the bar on the way to his office. Neither action would have been out of character for him in his duties as steward. All we've been able to establish is that he was not under observation for the entire time in question, so he *might* have had the opportunity to poison the port.

"So far, I've covered the seven members of the staff. And what has it told us? Just that we have seven people, each of whom had at least the possibility of entering the bar unobserved and placing the poison in the port. But not to leave anyone out, let's move on to the members.

"As you are all aware, the restroom facilities are adjacent to the bar next to the lounge. The most straight forward path to them from the dining room requires one to pass directly through the bar. This was obviously done for convenience and is in and of itself quite sensible. Also quite sensible is that after a lengthy dinner in which various liquid refreshments were served, some of the members would feel the need to attend to the call of nature. As the facilities are limited to a single toilet, this was done sequentially rather than *en mass*. By their own admission the following members went to the restroom and in this order, McAndrews, Fujika, Olberman, Nordlund, Kichler and Wu Lin. Each of them passed through the bar on their way, and while they were in the bar area they were alone. None of them can remember for certain whether the glass of port was sitting on the bar, but it seems likely that it was, so each of them had at least the possibility of access to the port.

"So what of the remaining members? Well Gordon by his own account walked through the bar on his way to the billiard room. He was alone at the time. DuChene left the dining room alone before the others to go to the lounge to make preparations for the bridge game that was to follow. He too walked through the bar while alone. Mr. Kasperovski, left the dining room headed for the library to work on some correspondence. On his way, he of course had to pass right by the bar, and of course, no one was in a position to see whether he entered the bar and poisoned the port.

"There we have it, gentlemen. And lady. Not a single person who was in the club that evening has an uninterrupted alibi during the interval that the port rested on the bar just waiting for someone to drop the cyanide into it. I find that fact quite remarkable. It's almost as if some clever individual had plotted things out just to make them difficult for the poor detective."

"I don't want to burst your bubble, Erik, but haven't you left one person out?" McAndrews asked with a hint of amusement.

"Have I? Yes, of course. His Excellency, Governor Tsangambo. You are quite right, sir. After the dinner, he made small talk with several of the members, tendered his compliments to the club steward Fenton, and then walked out of the dining room and left, walking down the corridor towards the front door, passing the bar on his way."

"Yes, you are correct inspector," the governor said with a touch of annoyance. "However, I distinctly remember Fenton standing at the door into the dining room watching me as I walked down the hall. Isn't that right?"

"Yes, of course, Governor," Fenton said. "But then I walked through the bar area on the way to my office. I didn't actually see you leave. I took a quick peek into the lounge on my way and when I reached the vestibule to turn into my office you weren't there. I had assumed that you had already exited through the door. But I suppose it is possible that you could have doubled back and headed to the bar unobserved by me."

"Surely you can't believe that?" the governor asked indignantly.

"Don't blame Fenton. He's only telling what he saw. We've no more reason to doubt your innocence than anyone else in the room tonight. However, just as with everyone else, there is no corroborating evidence indicating that you *did not* have the opportunity to poison the port. On those grounds, you must still be considered a suspect."

The governor hardly looked mollified.

"So, where does that leave us?" the inspector continued. "It would seem that our consideration of 'opportunity' has gotten us nowhere. We must look to 'motive' and hope that that will provide a solution."

CHAPTER 30
MOTIVE

"Almost from the beginning, I thought that it seemed likely that the motive behind the murder might well be found in something from Krieger's past. This line of investigation, however, presented some difficulties, largely because Peter Krieger seemed to be a man without a past. The investigation has been able to turn up nothing in the way of evidence that he even existed previous to his appearance in South America some fifteen years ago. No birth certificate, no educational records, no tax statements, nothing. Yet the man must have had a life prior to that point. He was, after all, around fifty years of age, a fact more or less confirmed by the autopsy. From his accent it would seem likely that he was a South African by birth, probably of Afrikaaner stock, an origin made more likely by the name of the mining company he founded, 'Pretoria Mining.' Yet a records search in South Africa and the surrounding countries has yielded no documentation of a Peter Krieger, at least not one of the right age who is not otherwise accounted for. The obvious conclusion is that the man known as 'Peter Krieger' had begun life under some other name and had changed it to conceal some fact or incident of his past life.

"Information of an indirect nature of Krieger's background was presented by a person who will, for the moment, remain nameless. This person stated that someone he knew had alleged that Krieger had been a leader of a group called 17 Commando which had been active during the Rhodesian War. 17 Commando, for those of you unfamiliar with the group, was aligned with the rebels who were trying to establish a white dominated state in what was then Zimbabwe. 17 Commando was also alleged to be responsible for any number of atrocities during the war both in Zimbabwe and in several neighboring countries. However, in the chaos that followed the collapse of the rebel movement, the leadership of 17 Commando vanished and has never been brought to justice. It is also rumored that the leadership, before they disappeared, had amassed a fortune, mostly in stolen diamonds, a fortune which also has never been recovered.

"Now, I want to make this clear," McKernan stated, "Peter Krieger's ties to 17 Commando and his identity as one of the leaders of that group have not been confirmed. It was a messy war and there is nothing in the form of tangible physical evidence such as fingerprints or DNA that can be used to positively I.D. any of the leadership of 17 Commando, and at this late date it is unlikely that any such evidence will ever turn up. All we have to go on is the hearsay report of a third party's opinion linking Krieger to 17 Commando.

"But whether Krieger was or was not a member of the group is irrelevant. What is important is that at least some people might have believed that he had been involved and that he bore responsibility for at least some of the atrocities committed during the war."

"Even granting that Krieger had been involved in the Rhodesian rebellion, I fail to see how this provides a motive, inspector," Wu Lin objected. "It was, after all, a long time ago and a world away."

"True. But it is in the nature of coincidence that unexpected links do occur. As it turns out, several people who were in the Mars Club that evening did have connections to that conflict despite the fact that it occurred nearly twenty years ago and as Mr. Wu Lin has said a world away.

"Perhaps the most obvious is the fact that Otis McAndrews, then a young mining engineer was part of a survey group that was attacked by 17 Commando. Otis was wounded, and along with another member of that party, was taken prisoner and held captive for a number of months. Otis was eventually rescued by government forces, but his friend, the friend who had nursed him during their captivity, was not so lucky having been shot to death, executed, as the rescue party closed in on the camp where they were being held. This much is public record as there are newspaper accounts of their capture by 17 Commando and their eventual recovery."

"Is this true, Otis?" Nordlund asked in surprise.

"Yes," McAndrews answered reluctantly.

"But you've never mentioned it!"

"I hope you can understand, it is not the sort of thing one likes to recall."

"I did ask Otis about the incident recently," McKernan said, resuming his narrative. "He claims that due to his wound he was delirious the entire time of his captivity and that while he was aware of the allegations, he can neither confirm or deny whether Krieger took part in the activities of 17 Commando. As I consider him a close friend and someone I greatly respect, I would like to believe him, but one has to admit that if Otis believed that Krieger was responsible for the death of his friend, he would have had a motive powerful enough to drive him to commit murder."

"You don't actually believe that, do you Erik?" McAndrews asked.

"I'm not accusing you, Otis, only stating that you may have had a motive," the inspector said quietly.

"But, it turns out," McKernan continued, "that by an odd quirk of fate that Otis was not the only one in the Mars Club that night affected by the violence of the Rhodesian War. Chef Duro had an older brother who was also a chef. He was working at a resort in Angola during the war, a country that was at peace at the time and not involved in the conflict. Unfortunately, 17 Commando, at least in the latter stages of the war, did not respect boundaries and made a number of incursions across the border in search of loot and supplies. Chef Duro's brother was killed in one of these raids. Now I have no reason to think that Chef Duro ever suspected that Krieger might have been one of the men responsible for his brother's death, but if he did, if, say, he had heard rumors of the fact, it is just possible that he too might be motivated to commit murder."

"Inspector, I did not do it," the chef protested. "I swear. I never heard anyone say that Mr. Krieger had been part of the rebels that killed my brother."

"Again, chef, I am not accusing you. I am only stating a possibility."

"Is this getting us anywhere, Inspector?" the governor asked.

"Perhaps, perhaps not, Governor," McKernan replied. "But in the name of fairness, I think it necessary to mention that you, yourself might have had a motive."

"You're going too far, McKernan."

"I mention this only as a possibility, and, I'm willing to admit, probably a remote one, but given your political beliefs you might be tempted to act if you believed Krieger was a white supremacist who had tried to exploit Africans."

"If I had believed that, I could easily have brought charges against him. The leadership of 17 Commando is still wanted for 'crimes against humanity,' you know," Tsangambo responded heatedly.

"But only if you had proof which you have denied having," McKernan countered.

"But to move on, I've given you three people who might possibly have had a motive stemming from the Rhodesian War. But there are also some more recent possibilities."

"Such as?" the governor asked.

"Some fifteen years ago, shortly after Krieger surfaced in South America there was a piece of gossip going around in Montevideo linking him to the wife of an Argentine mining engineer. The rumor even made it into one of the local gossip blogs. That engineer's name was Leo Kichler."

"Is that true, Leo?" Stan Olberman queried, waving his cocktail glass in the air.

"They were just rumors. Nothing ever happened," Kichler protested. "I was away for a month working on a new claim. We hadn't been married long. My wife was bored. She went out a few times with Krieger. But nothing more ever happened between them. She swore on her mother's grave. It was so long ago."

"I'm only listing the possibilities, Mr. Kichler," McKernan said quietly. "And there are others. Such as the one involving Mrs. Simpson, the housekeeper."

"Me? I'm sure you must be mistaken, inspector," Mrs. Simpson said, seemingly genuinely puzzled. "I had never even heard of Mr. Krieger before I came to Mars."

"No, but your husband was killed in an automobile accident. A hit and run. The driver of the car was never identified. Isn't that correct, Mrs. Simpson?"

"Yes. But as you say, the police were never able to trace the car."

"No, you are correct, not to the point of being able to bring charges. But they did have an idea of the make and the last three digits of the license plate number. It fit a vehicle owned by one Peter Krieger, who at the time was based out of London. However, he claimed that he was out of the country at the time and that his car was in Germany being repainted. The police had their suspicions, but they never had enough proof to make a case."

"But surely, even if this is true, you can't suspect me, inspector, can you?" Mrs. Simpson pleaded.

"It might not necessarily have been you, Mrs. Simpson. Mr. Duckworth might also have had motivation."

"Mr. Duckworth?" Mrs. Simpson asked, more confused than ever. "I'm afraid I don't understand, inspector. Why would Mr. Duckworth be involved."

"Perhaps he hasn't brought the subject up with you, but during his interview he mentioned a plan to open up a sort of resort hotel in the out there, and how he was looking for a partner, a partner in more than just business terms."

Mrs. Simpson flushing turned to look at the janitor. "You've never said a word, Walter."

Duckworth just looked embarrassed. He asked "But why would that make me want to kill Krieger?"

"Perhaps to win Mrs. Simpson's favor?" McKernan said, not without a trace of humor.

"This is becoming amusing, Inspector," the governor said. "Do you have any more little anecdotes to entertain us?"

"As a matter of fact, governor, yes I do, though perhaps with less grounds than those I've enumerated previously. Let's take the case of Mr. Teague, the bartender. I've already described how he certainly had the opportunity. The question is, did he have a motive?"

"Well, don't keep us waiting," Tsangambo protested.

"Krieger had accused him of stealing, wrongly as it developed, one of his precious bottles of port. The bottle in question was destroyed in transit, but that didn't keep Krieger from publicly accusing Teague of stealing it. He also complained to the club steward. Did Teague feel threatened? It's hard to say. Good bartenders are hard to come by on Mars, at least ones that understand premium liquor and wine. Krieger had also been known to use the term 'kafir' in reference to Mr. Teague behind his back. Grounds for resentment? Almost certainly. A motive for murder? Doubtful, at least for your average person in normal circumstances. But, is the situation on Mars normal?"

"And that brings us to Mr. Fenton. Krieger and he got into quite a shouting match over the damaged bottle of port. There are several independent witnesses to that. It appears Krieger also knew of the circumstances under which Fenton had been obliged to leave his previous position, certain financial irregularities with the club accounts which, while not traceable to Mr. Fenton, were his responsibility as steward of that club. Did Krieger threaten Fenton with this knowledge? Did Fenton feel that his position was in jeopardy? Did this amount to a motive for murder? Again, it's hard to say, but I feel that Mr. Fenton must be included on the list of those who might possibly have had a reason to wish Krieger dead."

"Aren't you leaving someone out, inspector?" the governor asked, his sense of humor seemingly restored.

"To whom are you referring to?" McKernan asked.

"Why William Watson, or as he is demeaningly referred to, Jeeves. Surely you've been able to concoct some implausible theory as to why he might have a motive. After all, you started this discussion with the claim that 'the butler did it,' as I remember."

"Happily, at least for Jeeves, I must say that try as I may I have been unable to come up with an obvious motive for Jeeves to wish to murder Krieger."

"Are we done then?"

"No. I'm afraid not. There is at least one other motive, a very common one. Money."

"Money? Have you discovered that under the terms of Krieger's will Kenji is going to inherit Pretoria Mining?" the governor quipped.

"No, but it is a fact that of the people at the dinner table, only Nordlund, DuChene, and yourself were not in direct competition with Pretoria Mining and by inference, Peter Krieger."

"I'm no proponent of the capitalist system, McKernan, but even to me that seems a rather broad assertion."

"Oh, I agree. I think that Mars is big enough to accommodate a little competition amongst the major mining corporations. In general, the relations between companies have tended to be cooperative rather than combative. Why, just the other day Otis was describing how Anglo-Martian often supplies lab services on a contract basis for some of its competitors."

"Then what was your point?" the governor asked impatiently.

"The question is, were any of the members at that dinner in a position where they saw either Krieger or Pretoria as a threat to their business or to their personal positions as executives of their respective companies?"

"And? Were they?"

"Due to the sensitive nature of that question, I think I will refrain from answering that question. At least for the moment. But I think we have to conclude that there is at least the possibility of a motive related to business for everyone except Nordlund and DuChene."

"So where does that put us, inspector? It seems that you've found a motive for everyone except Jeeves, Nordlund and DuChene. That doesn't seem to have moved things along much."

"Unfortunately, you are right. Which of course, brings us to the third part of the cliché, 'means'."

CHAPTER 31
MEANS

"Aren't you carrying this Hercule Poirot charade a bit far, Inspector?" the governor asked sarcastically. "Do you really have proof that one of the people in this room is guilty, or are you just bluffing in hopes that someone will break down and confess? I should think that most of us are far too intelligent for that trick to work. This is, after all, real life and not a detective novel."

"With all due respect, governor," Nordlund said quietly, "I think that as we've come this far, we should allow the Chief Inspector to finish. We owe it, if not to Peter Krieger's memory, at least to the notion that justice does have a place on Mars."

There was a murmur of assent and a nodding of heads from most of the group, though McKernan noticed that one member seemed to be sitting distinctly uneasily in his chair.

"Very well," Tsangambo acquiesced, "please continue, Inspector."

McKernan looked around the room and then resumed speaking:

"As I explained earlier, Krieger was poisoned by someone adding potassium cyanide to his glass of port, almost certainly while it sat on the bar during Teague's absence. We've already established that everyone who was in the club that night had access to the glass while they were unobserved. That line of investigation has proven to be a dead end in narrowing down the list of suspects.

However, there remains the question of how the murderer obtained the poison in the first place."

"The obvious thing was to search for traces of the poison on the person of the victim and in his suite in the club. If it had been found in either location, it would have meant that the possibility of suicide could not be ruled out. However, despite the best efforts of Dr. Greenwood and his staff and a thorough search of Krieger's suite, no trace of the poison was found.

"A search was also made of the rest of the Mars Club. Not surprisingly, no potassium cyanide has turned up. Now, I didn't really expect it to. Cyanide is not something that would be used in the normal day-to-day activities of the club. The conclusion we can draw from this is that the poison was brought into the club by the murderer specifically for the purpose of killing Peter Krieger. And because of that conclusion, his death becomes not a suicide, not a crime of passion, but a crime of premeditated murder."

McKernan had said the last with emphasis, and he took a moment to let it sink in with his listeners.

"The next question is, where did our murderer obtain the cyanide? After all, its properties as a poison are well known. One would surely think that it would be rare and tightly controlled in an environment as closed as Mars is. However, somewhat to my surprise, but then I'm no chemist, potassium cyanide is widely used in many industrial and scientific processes, especially in the mining and processing of minerals. Even a cursory investigation revealed that there were probably several metric tons of the stuff on Mars. Dr. Greenwood assures me that the amount of potassium cyanide that was required to poison Krieger was only a few grams.

"Fortunately, it seems that the various laboratories and other facilities that use potassium cyanide in their work *do* keep close tabs on their stocks and access is restricted and records are kept of the time and amount when any is requisitioned from their stockroom. One of the first things my department did when it was established that we were dealing with cyanide poisoning was to make inquiries of all the labs to see if any had gone missing."

"I should hope so, inspector," the governor jibed. "Even I would have thought of that. And I suppose that the replies came back saying that none was missing. Or that *all* of them were missing sufficient amounts. That would be about par for this case, wouldn't it?"

"You would be correct, your Excellency. That would be par for this case. Fortunately, none of the labs reported any missing cyanide, that is, except for one lab that reported about twenty five grams missing, more than enough, as it turns out, to have killed Krieger."

"And are you going to leave us in suspense or are you going to tell us which one?" Tsangambo queried.

"It was the assay lab of Anglo-Martian," McKernan announced firmly. His response created a stillness in the room while all eyes turned towards Otis McAndrews.

Fujika was the first to voice what was on everyone's mind. "You aren't implying that you think Otis is the murderer, are you Inspector? That's ridiculous."

"I'm not implying anything at the moment, Kenji. However, as my investigation has proceeded, the evidence, however circumstantial has tended to point in Otis's direction. First, he had the opportunity, though he is hardly unique in that respect. As to motive, well if in fact he believed that Krieger had been connected with 17 Commando, he would have had perhaps the strongest reason for wanting him dead. And as far as means go, it has been established that Otis was in the assay lab on the day that the cyanide went missing. He also, in the words of the laboratory technician in the lab is a 'very hands on kind of guy' well acquainted with the lab and its contents.

"But, what does this all mean? I have to admit that I found these facts troubling. Of all the people who were in the club that night, Otis is the one that I personally am closest to. Since I've been on Mars I've considered him a friend and even to some extent a mentor. There is no question that on several occasions he has proved helpful in solving crimes and in acting as an intermediary between my department and the corporations. I have been understandably reluctant to think of him as the killer.

"Did I, however, have any choice? Does the evidence prove he poisoned Krieger? Is it possible that he was being framed? Or, is the evidence, circumstantial as it is, just a coincidence. Fortunately, for the sake of our friendship, I've concluded that the latter is the case.

"Which brings us back to the original question of who killed Krieger? Is there another person who had the means, opportunity, and motive. I believe there is.

"Leaving aside the means and opportunity for the moment, let's consider motive. I have mentioned several facets of Krieger's past as possible motives, the unproven assertions of his membership in 17 Commando and his involvement in the death of Mrs. Simpson's husband. I think that we can rule out both of those as factors. I have no reason to believe that Mrs. Simpson was aware that Krieger had ever been a suspect in her husband's death. The police suspicions in this regards were never made public as their investigation was inconclusive. Nor do I believe that Chef Duro had any reason to think Krieger had anything to do with his brother's death. And, while the governor and

Otis might have had their suspicions, neither of them had any proof, and they are both far too wise to act without it."

"I appreciate the vote of confidence, inspector," the governor responded with a smile.

"That led me to the conclusion that the motive was due to something in the present, not the past. I think we can disregard the incident of the broken bottle of port. The evidence clearly indicates that the damage was done in transit and was not the fault of either Teague or Fenton, and while those individuals might have resented Krieger's accusations, those accusations were provably false, and that resentment would be a very weak motive for murder.

"So where does that leave us? That leaves us with money as the motive. Now, as I pointed out earlier, most of the members were in competition with Krieger and Pretoria Mining, but for all but one of those members that competition was not a matter of life or death. Certainly Anglo-Martian is and always has been on solid financial ground. The concessions of Celestial, Big Sky, and Fukashima are all solidly profitable. Siberian is perhaps less so, but still not in a desperate condition. Rio Plata is a more recent player, but there is no evidence that they are unhappy with their investment results so far."

While McKernan paused for a moment, he could see several of those present doing the mental arithmetic as to who was left.

"There is one company whose results lately have not been as satisfactory. Several concessions they have secured have definitely underperformed. This same company was in competition with Pretoria over a claim that if it was secured might reverse their fortunes, and with Krieger out of the way, the chances of securing that concession on affordable terms would be greatly enhanced."

Stan Olberman stood up a little unsteadily. "I see where this is going, McKernan. You think you can pin the murder on me rather than your friend McAndrews. Well. It won't work. You've got no evidence."

"Please sit down, Mr. Olberman," the inspector said firmly. "Several things have come to light. One is that Tranamerican is heavily overextended, overextended to the point that they are considering withdrawing from Mars altogether unless their operations here can be made profitable quickly. The management is not only unhappy with the local operation, but they have also become aware of your excessive drinking. Isn't it true that if they do withdraw from Mars you stand to lose your job?"

"It isn't my fault," Olberman pleaded. "I've had a run of bad luck. And what do you expect? I've been stuck in this godforsaken place for three years. Who wouldn't drink. But that doesn't mean I poisoned Krieger. You've got no proof of that. McKernan."

"Isn't it true that your personal finances are in pretty sad shape, Mr. Olberman? You are separated from your wife and facing a costly divorce settlement, you have two daughters approaching college age, and if you lose your job you'd be ruined?"

"Maybe that's all true. But you still have no proof that I killed Krieger."

"I wouldn't be so sure of that, Mr. Olberman. Something Otis mentioned got me to asking questions. He mentioned in passing that the corporations often cooperate. As an example he cited the fact that Anglo-Martian often does assays for other companies in their lab. It turns out that the day the cyanide went missing you had dropped in to check on the results of a sample, a sample. I might add, that proved to be worthless."

"So I was there. That doesn't mean I took the cyanide."

"No, it doesn't," McKernan agreed. "But for one incident. I was discussing the case with Otis in the lounge. He kindly ordered a round of Scotch from his private bottle. Unfortunately, we never drank the Scotch. It had been poisoned with cyanide. There was a note on the tray, a suicide note signed 'Otis McAndrews.' Otis didn't write that note.

"When I went to the bar after we had detected the poison, Teague said that the only one in the bar had been you. He said you had been writing something. He also said that you had asked for a fresh drink before Jeeves picked up the tray with the Scotches, and that his back was turned while he mixed it. You then drank your drink off in one gulp and left the bar. Is that correct, Mr. Olberman?"

"Maybe. I don't know. But it doesn't prove anything. Maybe your friend McAndrews tried poisoning you and got cold feet at the last second. Have you thought of that, Inspector?"

"No, I haven't, Mr. Olberman. The fact is, that when I had you quarters searched this morning we discovered traces of potassium cyanide in the pocket of the dinner jacket you wore last Friday. Stanley Olberman, I'm arresting you for the murder of Peter Krieger and for the attempted murders of Otis McAndrews and myself. Gaeretts, Ferris, take him away."

Olberman looked around him, but there was no place for him to go. Ferris grabbed his arms and handcuffed him.

After Olberman had been led through the airlock the governor remarked, "I have to admit, Chief Inspector, that this has all been very entertaining, perhaps the best evening I've had since I came to Mars. But was it really necessary? It was quite clear that you had made up your mind as to the guilty party and that you had enough evidence to make your case. Did you have to put us through this charade?"

"I wanted to make sure that I had the support of the men in this room. If I hadn't detailed my investigation, I'm not convinced that would be true. There was too much chance of second guessing. And, as I stated earlier, we have no institutions in place to handle such matters locally. If I had written up a report and sent it back to Earth along with Olberman could you guarantee that some clever lawyers wouldn't be able to set him free?"

"You've made your point, Chief Inspector," Tsangambo replied. "It is certainly something that will have to be considered. Are we done, then?"

"Yes, sir. My written report will be on your desk in the morning."

"Very good. Then, good evening, Chief Inspector. And thank you again for a most entertaining evening." The governor raised his hand in salute and departed.

Rather than breaking up, though, the event continued on as a party as those present discussed the case over drinks. There seemed a sense of relief that the uncertainties were over. Even Mrs. Simpson and Mr. Duckworth were seen having an earnest conversation off to the side.

The sun had set. Someone, probably Fenton, had turned down the lighting so that only some downward pointing LEDs around the rim were on. This provided enough light to see, but minimized any reflections from the inside surface of the dome allowing the stars to become visible. Off in the distance could be seen the spaceport where a shuttle was preparing to depart for a rendezvous with one of the interplanetary ships.

McAndrews came up to the inspector, scotch in hand. "Here my boy, you deserve this."

McKernan took the drink gratefully.

"I want to thank you, Erik. And not just for proving my innocence. I think your performance tonight made a very important point. There are some things that can't be left to the bureaucrats on Earth. They have to be handled here on Mars by the people that are directly affected. I've believed that all along, but I'm not sure that some of my colleagues were as convinced. I think tonight shows why matters of law and justice must be dealt with locally."

"I hope so, Otis. I really do. But we've been disappointed before."

They stood silent for a moment staring out at the Martian night. Kenji Fujika wandered by and joined them.

"There's one thing I want to know, Inspector. How could you be so sure that Otis wasn't the murderer? After all, you said yourself there was a lot of circumstantial evidence against him."

"Please, Erik. I'm interested, too," Otis said.

"Alright. Well, I could almost see Otis killing Krieger if he really thought that he had been part of 17 Commando. I could even see him deciding on suicide if he thought that there was no way out for him. What I couldn't see him doing is taking someone innocent with him. That's just not the Otis I've come to know."

"Thank you for that sentiment, Erik. I appreciate it," McAndrews said.

"Of course there is one other thing," McKernan said.

"Oh?" Kenji asked. "What's that?"

"If he had intended on committing suicide he would have used a cheaper scotch."

"There is that."

"Now, if you'll excuse me gentlemen, it's been a long night."

EPILOG

McKernan slipped out of the Cupola, went down the stairs to the main level and out the airlock to the Concourse. With that single step he felt he was back on the Mars that he knew. The Concourse, as sterile as it was, was familiar territory. For a moment he thought about returning to the police offices, but there was nothing there that really required his immediate attention. Gaeretts and Ferris could deal with Olberman. His formal report was already prepared and forwarding it to the governor could wait until morning. It was time to head home.

It was late enough that the Concourse was almost empty. The overhead lights had been turned to low and the scattered potted plants cast weird elongated shadows against the fused silica blocks of the walls. The lights on Finnegan's were turned off indicating that the place was closed and the owner had gone to bed. With a shrug, McKernan thought it was just as well.

He headed down the hallway that led to the Corridor C airlock as the quickest way home. Once through the lock, he wrapped his jacket tighter around him. The crisp, cold air of the Hut Town corridor seemed clean and fresh despite the ever present surface dust. One hundred meters up the corridor he went through another airlock and cut over through the cross tunnel into Corridor B.

As he exited the lock into the corridor he was above grade, with only the thin metal skin and a few centimeters of sprayed on foam insulation between him and the thin

Martian atmosphere. Another hundred meters of corridor, another airlock and he was almost home.

When he reached his front door, he entered the code to unlock it. He'd replaced the simple padlock with an electronic one when Beth had moved in so that she could lock the hatch when she was home and he was working. With a pang he wondered how much longer that would be a concern.

Once inside, he dropped his pistol in the basket by the lock. It was dark in the front room, with only the read-outs on the life support system and a digital clock providing illumination. It was 2432, only a few minutes before midnight.

He was surprised when, passing through the lock between the living room and the bedroom he found Beth still awake, reading in bed.

"Something good?" he asked as he hung up his jacket in the closet.

"A murder mystery. I think the butler did it."

"That's a myth. The butler is never the murderer."

"I guess that's why I'm a doctor and not a detective. How did it go tonight?"

"OK, I guess. I managed to convince them that Olberman was the killer. He broke down at the end."

"And Otis isn't under suspicion anymore?"

"No. That's one good thing that came out of tonight."

"You sound tired."

"It's been a long few days."

"But it's over now, isn't it?"

"It's over. For this case." He draped his pants and underwear on the bench at the foot of the bed and crawled beneath the covers. Since Beth had moved in he had kept the hut a few degrees warmer, but it was still chilly.

Beth turned off her reader and placed it on the nightstand.

"I heard from Earth today."

McKernan didn't have to ask about what.

"They've turned me down. The appointment went to someone else."

"I'm sorry to hear that," McKernan responded. "I know how much that meant to you." He realized that he did mean it. As much as he didn't want Beth to go back to Earth, he wanted her to be happy. He didn't want her to feel trapped. He also didn't want to ask her what her plans were because he was afraid of what the answer would be.

"I told Dr. Greenwood," Beth said. Greenwood was the head of the hospital. "He said they were having trouble finding a replacement for me." They both knew that was unlikely. Between the lack of job prospects on Earth and the pay premiums on Mars, there would always be qualified applicants. "He offered me a one year contract. Same pay and allowances and no strings. I think he just doesn't want to break in someone new."

McKernan could understand that. Even with the screening that was done thirty percent of people that came to Mars didn't work out and were shipped home before their three year contracts were up. But he also knew that if Beth had been ready to commit to a three year contract she would have been due a substantial bonus.

"I've decided to take it," Beth said when she realized that McKernan wasn't going to ask.

"I'm glad," McKernan said. They both knew that it didn't really change anything. Beth hadn't committed to Mars. McKernan would never go back. Could never go back. In a year they'd be facing the same question, but for now it didn't matter.

McKernan burrowed under the covers. Beth turned off the light and pressed herself up against him. Outside they could hear the wind as it drove the red dust of Mars against the thin skin of the hut.

AUTHOR'S AFTERWARD

Murder at the Mars Club is the fourth novel in the "Murder on Mars" series featuring Chief Inspector Erik McKernan, the previous entries being *The Blood Red Sands of Mars, A Death at Station Alpha,* and *A Corpse in Hut Town.* This series takes a variety of classic mystery plots and transports them to the Mars of the not too distant future where a small but dedicated security force tries to enforce the peace while coping with the planet's hostile environment.

Whereas in *A Death at Station Alpha,* McKernan must deal with a classic locked room mystery, in *Murder at the Mars Club* he is faced with the opposite problem, a case in which everyone present on the fateful evening had the opportunity to commit the crime. The crime itself, takes place within the confines of the Mars Club, a recreation of a London private club of the previous century complete with a butler who answers to the name "Jeeves." The Mars Club has made brief appearances in several of the previous novels in the series, but in this book, I explore the inner workings of the club in greater depth, contrasting its refined interior with the harsh world that waits just the other side of the airlock hatch.

As with the previous novels I have also used the book to explore issues related to the settling of another planet. The negotiations for allowing some sort of "home rule" for the residents of Mars, looms in the background, while certain forces wish to maintain the planet's colonial status. Not coincidentally, Earth's own colonial past figures in the mystery.

I've given Constable Ferris, who has appeared in several of the earlier novels, a greater role in this outing, serving as the foil to McKernan's musings on the crime. I also admit I've had a bit of fun with some of the trappings of classic British mysteries such as the compiling of a detailed timeline, the attempts to recreate the crime, and of course, most importantly, the final drawing room scene where the Inspector assembles all of the suspects to reveal the identity of the criminal.

For those fans of Constable Elena Ortiz who will notice her absence in this volume, she will return in the next book in the series, *A Body in the Dust,* where she will have her own mystery to solve while McKernan is preoccupied with other concerns. I've already completed the first few chapters and will soon be working full time on the new novel.

Greg Fowlkes

SPECIAL PREVIEW!

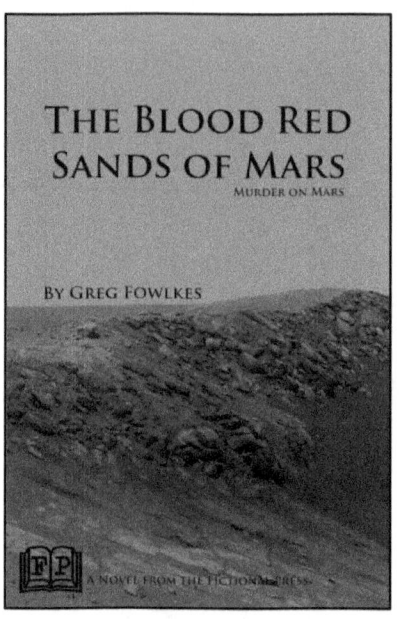

THE BLOOD RED SANDS OF MARS

By Greg Fowlkes

Book One from the Murder on Mars Series

Now available from The Fictional Press
www.TheFictionalPress.com

THE BLOOD RED SANDS OF MARS

The wind was blowing again against the west wall of the hut. He could hear the grains of sand abrading the thin aluminum skin that protected him from the outside. Through the window, half frosted from the continuous onslaught of sand and dust, he could see clouds of dust obscuring the sky. The sky was a pastel pink, a color no sky had any right to be. The wind, despite its 120 kph. velocity, made only a thin howl as it blew over the half buried cylinder of the hut.

McKernan lay on his cot trying not to admit that he was awake. It was a losing battle. After a few minutes he surrendered and glanced over at the clock sitting on the crate next to his bed. The dim red digits of the LED display read 7:58. It was too early to get up, too late to go back to sleep. He rolled over, shivering at the cold. The temperature couldn't have been more than ten degrees Celsius inside the hut. For the twentieth time he thought to himself that he would have to fix the heater before winter— if he could get the parts. Either that, or put in more insulation—if he could find that. The cold finally forced the decision to get up.

Standing, he felt the cold plastic floor beneath his bare feet. With his foot he fished the worn and patched pants from beneath the cot and pulled them on. He dug underneath his pillow and came up with a switchblade knife that he stuck in his pocket before drawing on the turtleneck sweater that had lain next to his pants. The cold feel of the cloth did nothing to dispel the cold from his body. From the crate he picked up a shoulder holster with a small automatic pistol and put it on. McKernan drew the weapon, worked the slide once, and after examining it perfunctorily, placed it back in the holster. Satisfied, he pulled on a worn pair of leather boots and placed another knife in a sheathe between his skin and the boot top.

Dressed, he went over to the shelf that served as counter and table. He put a pan of beans onto the heating unit and got a soysteak from the small refrigerator that held up one end of the shelf. The steak went into the frying pan on the other heating element. An egg would have been nice, but at the current price of three dollars apiece it was an extravagance that he would have to put off for a while.

As the food cooked he drew a liter of water from the spigot in the corner of the hut and watered the plants in the garden under the window. The carrots and tomatoes were doing nicely. He smiled briefly because it would be good to have fresh vegetables for a change. The big, leafy oxygen plants were doing well, too. He would be able to cut down on his oxygen ration this month and save some money.

He took the beans off the heating element and replaced them with the coffee pot. The beans were still half cold, but he wasn't in the mood to hassle with them. He only had the two heating elements, and he didn't want to have to wait for his coffee. He forced down the beans and then wolfed down the steak. It almost tasted like real beef, but then maybe his memories were fading. As usual, the coffee tasted terrible and tepid, too. The air pressure in the hut was too low for water to boil properly.

He finished his meal and scraped the remnants of food into the pressure vessel that served as a compost heap. The gauge on its neighbor showed that he had almost half a tank of methane. He'd be able to sell that soon and use the money for something useful, like a still. Completing his rounds, the gauges on the life support systems showed that everything was still working at keeping him alive. He went back to the pots and scrubbed them clean with sand. That, at least, was plentiful and cheap.

He checked his watch against the clock. It was time to get going. Pulling on his jacket he went to the airlock at the corridor end of the hut. After checking the gauge to make sure that there was pressure on the other side, he undogged the latches and stepped through. Closing the door behind him, he repeated the process with the outer hatch, latching both doors behind him. The outer door he locked with a heavy padlock.

He had entered a low tubular corridor made of the same aluminum foil and plastic foam construction as the hut. The walls, however, were even thinner, and no pretense was made of heating it. He could see his breath condensing in front of him as he began to walk down its length. It was a hell of a way to live, he reflected, not for the first time. But then, it had been hell living in L.A. where he'd been born, with brown air, rats, a chronic shortage of water, and overcrowded tenements. He had made his choice, but sometimes it seemed as though life was a continual shiver.

The corridor was pierced at regular intervals by hatches identical to his own. The huts behind the hatches were identical, too, except for the modifications the owners had made to make them more livable. This part of the city was old, dating back a couple of decades to the first days of the settlement when it had been part of a scientific base. The scientists had departed, at least from that corridor, and been replaced by those who had the money to buy or rent the huts from the Trust Authority. Maintenance was pretty much left up to the residents.

Along the sides and overhead ran the pipes and conduits that pumped in the gases, liquids, and power necessary for sustaining life. The whole system looked as jury rigged and fragile as it actually was, though surprisingly few people died whenever the system failed. Martians were a cautious lot. One didn't talk much about injuries. Accidents on Mars didn't leave many.

A hundred meters down the tube he came to an airlock. Going through the same ritual that he had used on his front door, he went through to another length of corridor indistinguishable from the one he had just left. Continuing on, he passed through two more airlocks until he entered a corridor that sloped downward. The hatches were farther apart, and larger. Signs overhead indicated the businesses or functions that were carried out behind them. The air was warmer because the corridor was buried beneath the sand which provided insulation. At the end of the tunnel was a larger airlock set into a wall of fused silica bricks, the first substantial piece of construction he had met that morning.

Passing through the portal was like entering another world, which in a way he had. This was the public Mars, the planet seen by the corporation men and the officials of the Trust Authority. It was also the planet seen by tourists, the brave new colony, man's first outpost on another planet. The tourists didn't really care to see the hut town. They were part of the same world as the corporation men and the government types. It still took a great deal of money or power to reach Mars.

The difference was more than one of degree. For one thing, the temperature was a comfortable twenty. For another, the walls were flat and met the floors and ceilings at right angles, unlike the inflated skins of the huts and corridors. With a little imagination it could almost be an enclosed shopping mall on earth, though the presence of fused silica blocks was more prevalent than any architect would allow.

The most important difference, however, was the sight of people scurrying along. He hadn't met anyone in the outer corridors. People rarely lingered there because of the cold. Now, McKernan could see at least twenty people and it was still fairly early. No airlocks interrupted this corridor. Extending for two hundred meters in either direction, it was twenty meters wide and ten high, the largest enclosed volume on the planet. Arrayed along its length were the offices and store fronts of the corporations that owned Mars, as well as the more prosperous saloons and bordellos.

One day the Trust Authority promised that the whole city would be like that, with apartments and condominiums for the ordinary workers, but neither the Authority or the corporations had yet come up with the money. For the moment all that existed was the one street of a few blocks.

McKernan headed towards the Authority's offices which dominated one end of the mall, but turned aside at the last moment when he noticed that a small, dark doorway was open. He knew that he should resist the temptation, but he was not in a very disciplined mood. He went through the doorway into the darkness beyond.

Finnegan's was the only real, honest bar on Mars. There were any number of saloons and even a cocktail lounge in the Mars Sheraton, but only one quiet, dark place where a man could drink in peace. McKernan felt the need for some of that peace at the moment.

He sat down on one of the stools before the only mahogany bar on Mars. Finnegan, himself, was behind the bar, though in fact he almost always was, no matter what the hour. The bartender looked up and greeted the newcomer, "Good morning, constable. Beer or whiskey?"

"It's too early for beer. It's too early for whiskey, but give me a shot, anyway."

Finnegan poured out a shot glass of amber liquid and placed it before McKernan and then stood back polishing a glass while he studied the man opposite him.

McKernan knocked back half the glass before he spoke. When he did, there was a bitter edge to his voice. "Sometimes I wonder if it's worth it, Finnegan. I could be back on a planet fit for human life."

"Could you, now, constable?" Finnegan said, putting down the glass and picking up another in equally gleaming condition. "If mother earth was such a bed of roses, why are you here?"

He breathed on the glass and examined it against the light for a moment, then looked at McKernan with the same intentness. "You're here because you're not the sort to live off the dole or to spend your life with another man being your boss. Instead you'll spend your life trying to make this planet a fit place to live and retire in twenty years with a nice pension. Now drink up and get to work, laddy."

"Yeah, sure. Sorry to burden you with my problems. Early morning depression, I guess. See you." He finished off the shot and left five dollars in Authority script on the bar.

The bite of the whiskey so early in the morning didn't really help his disposition, but it did give him enough courage to make it to the office. The morning ritual at Finnegan's was becoming too much of a habit. His three years on Mars were beginning to show.

The jail wasn't in the brick part of the Authority building, but in the complex of pneumatic architecture that sprawled behind it. The huts were old—older than his own—but dated back to the days when governments had not begrudged a few billions for exploration, back before space had to show a profit. For that reason, they were sound and well insulated, though a bit tacky looking.

The jail consisted of two huts joined together, one for offices, the other for the two makeshift cells and storage. Ferris was the only one there when he walked in, a young kid, younger than he had been himself when he had come to Mars. He was still impressed enough with his responsibilities and had not yet been worn down by the grim realities to take his job in any way but seriously.

Ferris greeted him with a solemn, "Good morning, sir," with a stress on the sir. As a three year veteran of Mars, Ferris looked on his boss with more than a touch of awe.

"Anything exciting happen overnight?" McKernan didn't really expect much. A few fights in the saloon district, a knifing maybe if things got out of hand. Petty thievery, or perhaps not so petty. He looked at Ferris and saw a flash of excitement in his eyes that the younger man was trying hard to suppress in order to match the hard bitten image he had of his superior.

"Yes, sir. We've got a murder on our hands."

"Another knifing down at Thelma's?" he asked, naming an infamous saloon and bordello that figured in a quarter of all the police reports.

"No. A prospector was found out on his claim yesterday, over on the far side of Olympus Mons. He was shot, Inspector."

That was bad, McKernan thought. People on Mars weren't supposed to have guns. With the thin skins of most buildings and a hostile atmosphere outside that would support life exactly as long as you could hold your breath, they were dangerous, and not just to the targets. The Authority had made them illegal and the corporations had been more than willing to agree. They weren't easy to get—not something that could be picked up casually or made, like a knife. Even without the details it sounded like the work of a real criminal and not just a squabble over a claim or a woman.

"Okay. Let me have the report. I'll take a look at it."

He took the folder from Ferris who looked a bit crestfallen. He probably expects me to go rush off to the outside and track down the murderer like an Indian scout, McKernan thought. He'd learn in time. Mars was a big planet and a dangerous one, but because of its nature there were also very few places that a man could run to and none where he could hide indefinitely.

He was leafing through the report when he came to his door. For the thousandth time he read, "Inspector Erik McKernan, Chief Constable." Mother would have been proud, he thought sardonically. She had hated the L.A. cops like all the other residents of the barrio. He went through the door into the little cubicle that was his real home. There, sitting at his desk, he began to read the report, sketchy though it was, to look for some explanations.

The Blood Red Sands of Mars c is available now from The Fictional Press. Find it on TheFictionalPress.com, or buy it on Amazon.com!

THE FICTIONAL DETECTIVE
BY GREG FOWLKES

WHO KILLED EZEKIAL O. HANDLER?

A beautiful dame, a hard-boiled private eye —- and a dead body.

It started like any other case. When a famous writer dies in a mysterious car crash, private detective Frank Slade is called in to find answers, but all he finds is more questions. Who killed Ezekial Handler? Who is Janet Nielsen and why is she so interested in finding out? Who is leaving the neatly typed clues? And as Slade tries to find answers to these questions he starts to wonder if the ultimate answer will threaten his very existence.

Now available from The Fictional Press.
Buy it on Amazon.com!

The Laws of Magic
By Greg Fowlkes

Egil Njalson was an aspiring lawyer. A lawyer with a difference. Not only had he passed the bar, but he had an undergraduate degree from the most prestigious school of magic in the country, the California Institute of Thaumaturgy. Needless to say his caseload and clients tended to the unusual. Like witches; or vampires. And the opposition, well they were likely to be demons. But Egil Njalson had sworn an oath to uphold the law of the land, and...

The Laws of Magic

Now available from The Fictional Press.
Buy it on Amazon.com!

BOOKS BY GREG FOWLKES

From the Wizard at Law Series:
The Laws of Magic
Trial by Magic

From the Murder on Mars Series:
Blood Red Sands of Mars
A Death at Station Alpha
A Corpse in Hut Town
Murder at the Mars Club

From the Fictional Detective Series:
The Fictional Detective
A Fictional Detective Trifecta

Star City Stories: Space Opera Noir Featuring Frank Sladek

The Uncorrupted Corpse

Tequila Visions

Cargo From Paradise

Ice Viking

The Fictional Press
www.TheFictionalPress.com

About The Fictional Press

The Fictional Press, an imprint of Intrepid Ink, LLC, provides full publishing services to authors of fiction and non-fiction books, eBooks and websites. From editing to formatting, to publishing, to marketing, Intrepid Ink gets your creative works into the hands of the people who want to read them.

Find out more at www.thefictionalpress.com.

www.ingramcontent.com/pod-product-compliance
Lightning Source LLC
Chambersburg PA
CBHW070104280626
47159CB00016B/1178